"I'M BLAISE HARMAN."

The voice was low and liquid. "And you're . . . Eric?"

Eric nodded, still blinking.

Yes, he's dazed all right, Thea thought. The *jerk*. She was surprised at her own vehemence.

"Good, because I wouldn't want to give this to the wrong person." Blaise produced the notebook from behind her back like a magician.

"Oh—where'd you get that?" Eric looked relieved and grateful. "I've been looking everywhere."

"My cousin gave it to me," Blaise said carelessly. She held onto the notebook as he tried to take it, and their fingers touched. "Wait. You owe me something for bringing it back, don't you?"

Her voice was a purr. And now Thea knew, without a doubt, what was going to happen.

Eric was doomed.

Done for, lost, a goner. Blaise had chosen him, and it was only a matter of how she was going to play him.

Books by L.J. Smith

THE FORBIDDEN GAME, VOLUME I: THE HUNTER
THE FORBIDDEN GAME, VOLUME II: THE CHASE
THE FORBIDDEN GAME, VOLUME III: THE KILL
DARK VISIONS, VOLUME I: THE STRANGE POWER
DARK VISIONS, VOLUME II: THE POSSESSED
DARK VISIONS, VOLUME III: THE PASSION
NIGHT WORLD: SECRET VAMPIRE
NIGHT WORLD: DAUGHTERS OF DARKNESS
NIGHT WORLD: SPELLBINDER

Available from ARCHWAY Paperbacks

L.J. SMITH

NIGHT WORLD™

Spellbinder

AN ARCHWAY PAPERBACK
Published by POCKET BOOKS
New York London Toronto Sydney Tokyo Singapore

AN ARCHWAY PAPERBACK *Original*

An Archway Paperback published by
POCKET BOOKS, a division of Simon & Schuster Inc.
1230 Avenue of the Americas, New York, NY 10020

ISBN: 0-671-55135-3

First Archway Paperback printing October 1996

10 9 8 7 6 5 4 3 2 1

NIGHT WORLD is a trademark of Lisa J. Smith

AN ARCHWAY PAPERBACK and colophon are registered trademarks of Simon & Schuster Inc.

Cover art by Sanjulian

Printed in the U.S.A.

IL 7+

For Maurice Ogden, with thanks

The Night World . . . love was never so scary.

The Night World isn't a place. It's all around us. It's a secret society of vampires, werewolves, witches, and other creatures of darkness that live among us. They're beautiful and deadly and irresistible to humans. Your high school teacher could be one, and so could your boyfriend.

The Night World laws say it's okay to hunt humans. It's okay to toy with their hearts, it's even okay to kill them. There are only two things you can't do with them.

  1) Never let them find out the Night World exists.
  2) Never fall in love with one of them.

These are stories about what happens when the rules get broken.

1

Expelled.

It was one of the scariest words a high school senior could think of, and it kept ringing in Thea Harman's mind as her grandmother's car approached the school building.

"This," Grandma Harman said from the front passenger seat, "is your last chance. You do realize that, don't you?"

As the driver pulled the car to the curb, she went on. "I don't know why you got thrown out of the last school, and I don't want to know. But if there's one *whiff* of trouble at this school, I'm going to give up and send both of you to your Aunt Ursula's. And you don't want *that*, now, do you?"

Thea shook her head vigorously.

Aunt Ursula's house was nicknamed the Convent, a gray fortress on a deserted mountaintop. Stone walls everywhere, an atmosphere of gloom—and Aunt Ursula watching every move with thin lips. Thea would rather die than go there.

In the backseat next to her, Thea's cousin Blaise was shaking her head, too—but Thea knew better than to hope she was listening.

Thea herself could hardly concentrate. She felt dizzy and very untogether, as if half of her were still back in New Hampshire, in the last principal's office. She kept seeing the look on his face that meant she and Blaise were about to be expelled—again.

But this time had been the worst. She'd never forget the way the police car outside kept flashing red and blue through the windows, or the way the smoke kept rising from the charred remains of the music wing, or the way Randy Marik cried as the police led him off to jail.

Or the way Blaise kept smiling. Triumphantly, as if it had all been a game.

Thea glanced sideways at her cousin.

Blaise looked beautiful and deadly, which wasn't her fault. She always looked that way; it was part of having smoldering gray eyes and hair like stopped smoke. She was as different from Thea's soft blondness as night from day and it was her beauty which kept getting them in trouble, but Thea couldn't help loving her.

After all, they'd been raised as sisters. And the sister bond was the strongest bond there was . . . to a witch.

But we can't get expelled again. We can't. *And I know you're thinking right now that you can do it all over again*

*and good old Thea will stick with you—but this time
you're wrong. This time I've got to stop you.*

"That's all," Gran said abruptly, finishing with her
instructions. "Keep your noses clean until the end of
October or you'll be sorry. Now, get out." She
whacked the headrest of the driver's seat with her
stick. "Home, Tobias."

The driver, a college-age boy with curly hair who
had the dazed and beaten expression all Grandma's
apprentices got after a few days, muttered, "Yes, High
Lady," and reached for the gearshift. Thea grabbed
for the door handle and slid out of the car fast. Blaise
was right behind her.

The ancient Lincoln Continental sped off. Thea was
left standing with Blaise under the warm Nevada sun,
in front of the two-story adobe building complex.
Lake Mead High School.

Thea blinked once or twice, trying to kick-start her
brain. Then she turned to her cousin.

"Tell me," she said grimly, "that you're not going
to do the same thing here."

Blaise laughed. "I never do the same thing twice."

"You know what I *mean.*"

Blaise pursed her lips and reached down to adjust
the top of her boot. "I think Gran overdid it a little
with the lecture, don't you? I think there's something
she's not telling us about. I mean, what was that bit
about the end of the month?" She straightened,
tossed back her mane of dark hair and smiled
sweetly. "And shouldn't we be going to the office to
get our schedules?"

"Are you going to answer my *question?*"

"Did you ask a question?"

Thea shut her eyes. "Blaise, we are running out of relatives. If it happens again—well, do *you* want to go to the Convent?"

For the first time, Blaise's expression darkened. Then she shrugged, sending liquid ripples down her loose ruby-colored shirt. "Better hurry. We don't want to be tardy."

"You go ahead," Thea said tiredly. She watched as her cousin walked away, hips swaying in the trademark Blaise lilt.

Thea took another breath, examining the buildings with their arched doorways and pink plaster walls. She knew the drill. Another year of living with *them*, of walking quietly through halls knowing that she was different from everybody around her, even while she was carefully, expertly pretending to be the same.

It wasn't hard. Humans weren't very smart. But it took a certain amount of concentration.

She had just started toward the office herself when she heard raised voices. A little knot of students had gathered at the edge of the parking lot.

"Stay away from it."

"Kill it!"

Thea joined the periphery of the group, being inconspicuous. But then she saw what was on the ground beyond the curb and she took three startled steps until she was looking right down at it.

Oh . . . how *beautiful*. Long, strong body . . . broad head . . . and a string of rapidly vibrating horny rings on the tail. They were making a noise like steam escaping, or melon seeds being shaken.

The snake was olive green, with wide diamonds down its back. The scales on the face looked shiny, almost wet. And its black tongue flickered so fast. . . .

A rock whizzed past her and hit the ground beside the snake. Dust puffed.

Thea glanced up. A kid in cutoffs was backing away, looking scared and triumphant.

"Don't do that," somebody said.

"Get a stick," somebody else said.

"Keep away from it."

"Kill it."

Another rock flew.

The faces around Thea weren't vicious. Some were curious, some were alarmed, some were filled with a sort of fascinated disgust. But it was all going to end up the same for the snake.

A boy with red hair came running up with a forked branch. People were reaching for rocks.

I can't let them, Thea thought. Rattlers were actually pretty fragile—their backbones were vulnerable. These kids might kill the snake without even meaning to.

Not to mention that a couple of the kids might get bitten in the process.

But she didn't have anything . . . no jasper against venom, no St. John root to soothe the mind.

It didn't matter. She had to do *something*. The redheaded boy was circling with the stick like a fighter looking for an opening. The kids around him were alternately warning him and cheering him on. The snake was swelling its body, tongue-tips flickering up and down faster than Thea's eye could follow. It was *mad*.

Dropping her backpack, she slipped in front of the red-haired boy. She could see his shock and she heard several people yell, but she tried to block it all out. She needed to focus.

I hope I can do this. . . .

She knelt a foot away from the rattler.

The snake fell into a striking coil. Front body raised in an S-shaped spiral, head and neck held like a poised javelin. *Nothing* looked so ready to lunge as a snake in this position.

Easy . . . easy, Thea thought, staring into the narrow catlike pupils of the yellow eyes. She slowly lifted her hands, palms facing the snake.

Worried noises from the crowd behind her.

The snake was inhaling and exhaling with a violent hiss. Thea breathed carefully, trying to radiate peace.

Now, who could help her? Of course, her own personal protector, the goddess closest to her heart. Eileithyia of ancient Crete, the mother of the animals.

Eileithyia, Mistress of the Beasts, please tell this critter to calm *down*. Help me see into its little snaky heart so I'll know what to do.

And then it happened, the wonderful transformation that even Thea didn't understand. Part of her *became* the snake. There was a strange blurring of Thea's boundaries—she was herself, but she was also coiled on the warm ground, angry and excitable and desperate to get back to the safety of a creosote bush. She'd had eleven babies some time ago and had never quite recovered from the experience. Now she was surrounded by large, hot, fast-moving creatures.

Big-living-things . . . way too close. Not responding to my threat noises. Better bite them.

The snake had only two rules for dealing with animals that weren't food. 1) Shake your tail until they go away without stepping on you. 2) If they don't go away, strike.

Thea the person kept her hands steady and tried to pound a new thought into the small reptile brain. *Smell me. Taste me. I don't smell like a human. I'm a daughter of Hellewise.*

The snake's tongue brushed her palm. Its tips were so thin and delicate that Thea could hardly feel them flicker against her skin.

But she could feel the snake drop down from maximum alert. It was relaxing, ready to retreat. In another minute it would listen when she told it to slither away.

Behind her, she heard a new disturbance in the crowd.

"There's Eric!"

"Hey, Eric—rattlesnake!"

Block it out, Thea thought.

A new voice, distant but coming closer. "Leave it alone, guys. It's probably just a bull snake."

There was a swell of excited denial. Thea could feel her connection slipping. Stay focused. . . .

But nobody could have stayed focused during what happened next. She heard a quick footstep. A shadow fell from the east. Then she heard a gasp.

"Mojave rattler!"

And *then* something hit her, sending her flying sideways. It happened so fast that she didn't have time to twist. She landed painfully on her arm. She lost control of the snake.

All she could see as she looked east was a scaly olive-green head driving forward so fast it was a blur. Its jaws were wide open—amazingly wide—and its fangs sank into the blue-jeaned leg of the boy who had knocked Thea out of the way.

CHAPTER

2

The crowd erupted in panic.

Everything was happening at once; Thea couldn't sort out the different impressions. Half the people in front of her were running. The other half were yelling.

"Call nine-one-one—"

"It got Eric—"

"I *told* you to kill it!"

The red-headed boy was darting forward with his stick. Other kids were rushing around, looking for rocks. The group had become a mob.

The snake was rattling wildly, a terrifying sizzling sound. It was in a frenzy, ready to strike again at any moment—and there was nothing Thea could do.

"Hey!" The voice startled her. It came from Eric, the boy who'd been bitten. "Calm down, you guys. Josh, give me that." He was talking to the redhead with the forked branch. "It didn't bite me. It just struck."

Thea stared at him. Was this guy *crazy?*

But people were listening to him. A girl in baggy shorts and a midriff top stopped hefting her rock.

"Just let me get hold of it . . . then I can take it out into the brush where it won't hurt anybody."

Definitely crazy. He was talking in such a matter-of-fact, reasonable way—and he was going to try to pin the snake down with that stick. *Somebody* had to act fast.

A flash of ruby-color caught Thea's eye. Blaise was in the crowd, watching with pursed lips. Thea made her decision.

She dove for the snake.

It was watching the stick. Thea grabbed for its mind before grabbing its body—which kept it immobilized for the instant she needed to seize it just below the head. She hung on while its jaws gaped and its body lashed.

"Grab the tail and we'll get it out of here," she said breathlessly to Eric the crazy guy.

Eric was staring at her grip on the snake, dumbfounded. "For God's sake, don't let go. It can twist in a second. . . ."

"I know. *Grab* it!"

He grabbed it. Most of the crowd scattered as Thea wheeled around with the snake's head held tightly at arm's length. Blaise didn't run, she just looked at the snake as if it smelled bad.

"I need this," Thea whispered hastily as she passed her cousin. She snatched at Blaise's necklace with her free hand. The fragile gold chain broke and Thea's fingers closed around a stone.

Then she was heading out into the scrub brush, the weight of the snake dragging on her arm. She walked fast, because Eric didn't have much time. The grounds behind the school sloped up and then downward, getting wilder and more gray-brown. When the buildings were out of sight, Thea stopped.

"This is a good place," Eric said. His voice was strained.

Thea glanced back and saw that he looked pale. Brave and very, very crazy, she thought. "Okay, we let go on three." She jerked her head. "Throw it that way and back up fast."

He nodded and counted with her. "One . . . two . . . *three.*"

Giving it a slight swing, they both let go. The snake flew in a graceful arc and landed near a clump of purple sage. It wriggled immediately into the brush without showing the slightest hint of gratitude. Thea felt its cool, scaly mind recede as it thought, *That smell . . . that shade . . . safety.*

She let out the breath she hadn't realized she'd been holding.

Behind her, she heard Eric sit down abruptly. "Well, that's that." His own breathing was fast and irregular. "Now could I ask you a favor?"

He was sitting with his long legs straight out, his skin even paler than before. Perspiration beaded on his upper lip.

"You know, I'm not really sure it didn't bite me," he said.

Thea knew—and knew Eric knew—that it *had.* Rattlers did sometimes strike without biting, and did sometimes bite without injecting venom. But not this time. What she couldn't believe was that any human would care enough about a snake to let a bite go untreated.

"Let me see your leg," she said.

"Actually, I think maybe you'd better just call the paramedics."

"Please let me see." She kept her voice gentle, kneeling in front of him, reaching slowly. The way she'd approach a scared animal. He held still, letting her roll up his jeans leg.

There it was, the little double wound in the tanned skin. Not much blood. But surrounded by swelling already. Even if she ran back to the school, even if the paramedics broke every speed law, it wouldn't be fast enough. Sure, they'd save his life, but his leg would swell up like a sausage and turn purple and he'd have days of unbelievable pain.

Except that Thea had in her hand an Isis bloodstone. A deep red carnelian engraved with a scarab, symbol of the Egyptian Queen goddess, Isis. The ancient Egyptians had put the stones at the feet of mummies; Blaise used it to heighten passion. But it was also the most powerful purifier of the blood in existence.

Eric groaned suddenly. His arm was over his eyes, and Thea knew what he must be feeling. Weakness, nausea, disorientation. She felt sorry for him, but his confusion would actually work to her advantage.

She pressed her hand to the wounds, the carnelian

hidden between her tightly closed fingers. Then she started to hum under her breath, visualizing what she wanted to happen. The thing about gems was that they didn't work on their own. They were just a means of raising psychic power, focusing it, and directing it to a certain purpose.

Find the poison, surround it, dispel it. Purify and eliminate. Then encourage the body's natural defenses. Finally, soothe away the swelling and redness, sending the blood back where it belonged.

As she knelt there, feeling the sun on the back of her head, she suddenly realized that she'd never done this before. She'd healed animals—puppies with toad poisoning and cats with spider bites—but never a person. Funny how she'd known instinctively that she could do it. She'd almost felt that she *had* to do it.

She sat back on her heels, pocketing the bloodstone. "How are you feeling?"

"Huh?" He took his arm away from his eyes. "Sorry—I think I sort of blanked out there for a minute."

Good, Thea thought. "But how do you feel now?"

He looked at her as if he were struggling under pressure to be gentle. He was going to explain to her that people who got bitten by rattlesnakes felt sick. But then his expression changed. "I feel . . . it's weird . . . I think maybe it's gone numb." He peered doubtfully at his calf.

"No, you were just lucky. You didn't get bitten."

"*What?*" He scrambled to roll his jeans leg up higher. Then he just stared. The flesh was smooth and unmarked, with just the slightest trace of redness left. "I was sure . . ."

He lifted his eyes to hers.

It was the first time Thea had really gotten a chance to look at him. He was a nice-looking guy, lean and sandy-haired and sweet-faced. Long legs. And those eyes . . . deep green with gray flecks. Just now they were both intense and bewildered, like those of a startled kid.

"How'd you do that?" he said.

Thea was shocked speechless.

He wasn't supposed to respond like this. What was wrong with him? When she could talk again, she said, "I didn't do anything."

"Yes, you did," he said, and now his eyes were clear and direct, full of an odd conviction. Suddenly his expression changed to something like wonder. "You . . . there's something so different about you."

He leaned forward slowly, as if entranced. And then . . . Thea experienced an odd duality. She was used to seeing herself through the eyes of animals: a big, hairless creature in false skins. But now she saw herself as Eric saw her. A kneeling girl with yellow hair falling loose over her shoulders and soft brown eyes. A face that was too gentle, with a very worried expression.

"You're . . . beautiful," Eric said, still wondering. "I've never seen anybody . . . but it's like there's a mist all around you. You're so mysterious. . . ."

A huge quivering stillness seemed to hang over the desert. Thea's heart was beating so hard that it shook her body. *What was happening?*

"It's like you're part of everything out here," he said in that wise, childlike voice. "You belong to it. And there's so much peace. . . ."

"*No,*" Thea said. There was no peace at all in her. She was terrified. She didn't know what was going on, but she knew she had to get away.

"Don't go," he said, when she shifted. He had the stricken expression of a heartbroken puppy.

And then . . . he reached for her. Not roughly. His fingers didn't close on her wrist. They just brushed the back of her hand, sliding away when she jerked.

But it didn't matter. That light touch had raised all the hairs on Thea's forearm. And when she looked back into the gray-flecked green eyes, she knew he'd felt it, too.

A sort of piercing sweetness, a dizzying exhilaration. And—a connection. As if something deeper than words was being communicated.

I know you. I see what you see. . . .

Almost without knowing what she was doing, Thea raised her hand. Fingertips slightly outspread, as if she were going to touch a mirror or a ghost. He brought his hand up, too. They were staring at each other.

And then, just before their fingers made contact, Thea felt a jolt of panic like ice water.

What was she *doing?* Had she lost her mind?

Suddenly everything was clear—too clear. Her future stretched out before her, every detail sharp. Death for breaking Night World law. Herself centered in the Inner Circle, trying to explain that she hadn't meant to betray their secrets, that she hadn't meant to . . . to get close to a human. That it was all a mistake, just a moment of stupidity because she'd wanted to heal him. And them bringing the Cup of Death anyway.

The vision was so clear it seemed like a prophecy. Thea jumped up as if the ground had lurched underneath her, and she did the only thing she could think of to do.

She said scathingly, "Are you *nuts?* Or is your brain just overheated or something?"

He got the stricken look again.

He's a human. One of *them*, Thea reminded herself. She put even more scorn in her voice. "I'm part of everything; I did something to your leg . . . yeah, sure. I bet you believe in Santa Claus, too."

Now he looked shocked—and uncertain. Thea went for the coup de grâce. "Or were you just trying to put the moves on me?"

"Huh? *No*," he said. He blinked and looked around. The desert was the ordinary desert, gray-green and parched and flat. Then he looked at his leg. He blinked again, as if getting a fresh grip on reality. "I . . . look, I'm sorry if I upset you. I don't know what's wrong with me."

Suddenly he gave a sheepish smile. "Maybe I'm kind of weird from being scared. I guess I'm not as brave as I thought."

Relief trickled through Thea. He was buying it. Thank Isis that humans were stupider than chickens.

"And I wasn't trying to move in on you. I just—" He broke off. "You know, I don't even know your *name*."

"Thea Harman."

"I'm Eric Ross. You're new here, aren't you?"

"Yes." Stop talking and *go*, she ordered herself.

"If I can show you around or anything . . . I mean,
I *would* like to see you again. . . ."

"No," Thea said flatly. She would have liked to
have kept it to that monosyllable, but she wanted to
crush this new idea of his completely. "I don't want
to see *you*," she said, too rattled to think of any more
subtle way to put it.

And then she turned and walked away. What else
was there to do? She certainly couldn't talk to him
anymore. Even if she would always wonder why
he'd been crazy enough to care about the snake, she
couldn't ask. From now on she had to stay as far
away from him as possible.

She hurried back to the school—and realized immediately that she was late. The parking lot was quiet.
Nobody was walking outside the adobe buildings.

On my first day, too, Thea thought. Her backpack
was on the ground where she'd dropped it, a notebook lying beside it on the asphalt. She grabbed them
both and all but ran to the office.

It was only in physics class, after she'd handed her
admission slip to the teacher and walked past rows
of curious eyes to an empty seat in the back, that
she realized the notebook wasn't hers.

It fell open to a page that had *Introduction to Flatworms* scribbled in sloping, spiky blue ink. Below
were some pictures labeled *Class Turbellaria* and *Class
Trematoda*. The worms were beautifully drawn, with
their nervous systems and reproductive organs

1 7

shaded in different colors of highlighter, but the artist had also given them big goofy smiling faces. Grotesque but lovable in a cross-eyed way. Thea turned the page and saw another drawing, the *Life Cycle of the Pork Tapeworm.*

Yum.

She leafed back to the beginning of the notebook. *Eric Ross, Honors Zoology I.*

She shut the book.

Now how was she going to get it back to him?

Part of her mind worried about this through physics and her next class, computer applications. Part of it did what it always did at a new school, or any new gathering of humans: it watched and cataloged, keeping alert for danger, figuring out how to fit in. And part of it simply said, I didn't know they had a zoology class here.

The one question she *didn't* want to ask herself was what had happened out there in the desert? Whenever the thought came up, she pushed it away brusquely. It must have had something to do with her senses being too open after merging with the snake.

Anyway, it hadn't meant anything. It had been a weird one-time fluke.

In the main hallway at break, Blaise came rushing up, quick as a lioness despite the high heels.

"How's it going?" Thea said, as Blaise drew her into a temporarily deserted classroom.

Blaise just held out her hand. Thea fished in her pocket for the carnelian.

"You ruined the chain, you know," Blaise said as

she shook back midnight hair and examined the stone for damage. "And it was one I designed."

"Sorry. I was in a hurry."

"Yes, and *why*? What did you want with it?" Blaise didn't wait for a response. "You healed that boy, didn't you? I knew he got bitten. But he was *human*."

"Reverence for life, remember?" Thea said. " 'An ye harm none, do as you will." She didn't say it with much conviction.

"That doesn't mean humans. And what did he *think*?"

"Nothing. He didn't know I was healing him; he didn't even realize he got bitten." It wasn't *exactly* a lie.

Blaise looked at her with smoky, suspicious gray eyes. Then she glanced heavenward and shook her head. "Now if you'd been using it to *heat* his blood, I'd understand. But maybe you were doing a little of that, too. . . ."

"No, I was *not*," Thea said. And despite the warmth that rose in her cheeks her voice was cold and sharp. The horror of that death vision was still with her. "In fact, I don't ever want to see him again," she went on jaggedly, "and I told him so, but I've got his stupid *notebook*, and I don't know what to do with it." She waved the notebook in Blaise's face.

"Oh." Blaise considered, head on one side. "Well . . . *I'll* take it to him for you. I'll track him down somehow."

"Would you?" Thea was startled. "That's really nice."

"Yes, it is," Blaise said. She took the notebook, handling it carefully, as if her nails were wet. "Okay, well, I'd better get to my next class. Algebra." She made a face. " 'Bye now."

Suspicion struck as Thea watched her go.

Blaise wasn't usually so accommodating. And that " 'bye now" . . . too sweet. She was up to something.

Thea followed the ruby of Blaise's shirt as Blaise went back into the main hallway, then turned without hesitation into a locker-lined corridor. There, searching through one of the lockers, was a lean figure with long legs and sandy hair.

Fastest tracking I've ever seen, Thea thought sourly. She peered around the Mediterranean-blue door of a broken locker.

Blaise walked up behind Eric very slowly, hips swaying. She put a hand on his back.

Eric jumped slightly, then turned around.

Blaise just stood there.

It was all she needed to do. Blaise reeled guys in just by *being*. It was the glorious dark hair, the smoldering gray eyes . . . plus a figure that could stop traffic on the freeway. Curves galore, and clothes that emphasized every one. On another girl it might have been too much, but on Blaise it was just breathtaking. Guys who thought they liked the waif look dropped everything to follow her just as fast as guys who thought they liked blonds.

Eric blinked at her, looking hazy already. He didn't seem to know what to say.

That wasn't unusual. Guys always got tongue-tied around Blaise.

"I'm Blaise Harman." The voice was low and liquid. "And you're . . . Eric?"

Eric nodded, still blinking.

Yes, he's dazed all right, Thea thought. The *jerk*. She was surprised at her own vehemence.

"Good, because I wouldn't want to give this to the wrong person." Blaise produced the notebook from behind her back like a magician.

"Oh—where'd you get that?" Eric looked relieved and grateful. "I've been looking everywhere."

"My cousin gave it to me," Blaise said carelessly. She held onto the notebook as he tried to take it, and their fingers touched. "Wait. You owe me something for bringing it back, don't you?"

Her voice was a purr. And now Thea knew, without a doubt, what was going to happen.

Eric was doomed.

CHAPTER

3

Done for, lost, a goner. Blaise had chosen him, and it was only a matter of how she was going to play him.

A parade of names marched through Thea's mind. Randy Marik. Jake Batista. Kristoffer Milton. Troy Sullivan. Daniel Xiong.

And now: Eric Ross.

But Eric was talking, sounding animated. "Your cousin? Is she that other new girl? Thea?"

"Yes. Now—"

"Look, do you know where she is? I really want to talk to her." The hazy look descended again, and Eric stared into the distance. "She's just . . . I've never met anybody like her. . . ."

Blaise let go of the notebook and stared.

From her hiding place, Thea stared, too.

It had never happened before. This guy didn't even seem to *see* Blaise.

That was strange enough. But by the Blue Monkey-headed Goddess of Inquisitiveness, what Thea really wanted to know was why she herself felt so relieved by it.

A bell rang. Blaise was still standing there flabbergasted. Eric stuffed the notebook in his backpack.

"Could you just let her know I asked about her?"

"She doesn't *care* if you asked about her!" Blaise snapped, voice no longer honeyed. "She said very explicitly that she never wanted to see you again. And I'd watch out if I were you. Because she has a *temper*." The last word was uttered in rising tones.

Eric looked slightly alarmed—and crestfallen. Thea saw his throat move as he swallowed. Then, without saying good-bye to Blaise, he turned and walked out the far side of the corridor.

Well, by the Red Crow-headed Thunderbolt Goddess. Blaise turned around and stalked up the corridor in Thea's direction. Thea didn't even try to hide.

"So you saw all that. Well, I hope you're happy," Blaise said waspishly.

Thea wasn't. She was confused. Strangely agitated—and *scared*, because the Cup of Death was still floating before her eyes.

"I guess we should both just leave him alone," she said.

"Are you kidding? I'm going to *have* him," Blaise said. "He's *mine*. Unless," she added, eyes glittering, "you've already staked a claim."

Thea floundered, shocked. "I . . . well, no . . ."

"Then he's mine. I like a challenge." Blaise ran a hand through her hair, disordering the black waves. "Isn't it nice that Gran has so many love charms in the shop," she mused.

"Blaise . . ." Thea had a hard time collecting her thoughts. "Don't you *remember* what Gran said? If there's any more trouble . . ."

"There isn't going to be any trouble for *us*," Blaise said, her voice flat and positive. "Only for *him*."

Thea walked to her next class feeling oddly empty. Ignore it, she thought. There's nothing you can do.

She didn't see many Night People along the way to class. A young kid, probably a freshman, who looked like a shapeshifter; a teacher who had the hunting light of the lamia—the born vampires—in his eyes. No made vampires, no werewolves. No other witches.

Of course, she couldn't be certain. All the people of the Night World were masters of secrecy, of blending in, of passing unseen. They had to be. It was what allowed them to survive in a world where there were so many more humans . . . and where humans loved to kill anything different.

But when she was sitting in the world literature classroom, Thea noticed a girl in the next row.

The girl was small-boned and pretty, with thick eyelashes and hair as black and soft as soot. She had a heart-shaped face—and dimples. But what caught Thea's eye was the girl's hand, which was playing with a pin on the girl's blue-and-white-striped vest. A pin in the shape of a black flower.

A dahlia.

Thea immediately turned to a blank page in her notebook. While the teacher read a passage from the story *Rashomon*, Thea began drawing a black dahlia, tracing it over and over until it was large enough for the girl to see distinctly. When she raised her head, she saw the girl was looking at her.

The girl's lashes swept down as she looked at the drawing, then up again. She smiled at Thea and nodded slightly.

Thea smiled and nodded back.

After class, without any need to discuss it, Thea followed the girl to the front of the school. The girl looked around to make sure no one was in earshot, then turned to Thea with something like resigned wistfulness.

"Circle Midnight?" she said.

Thea shook her head. "Circle Twilight. Aren't you?"

The girl's face lit up with shy delight. Her eyes were dark and velvety. "Yes!" she said and rushed on, "But there are only two more of us—two seniors, I mean—and they're both Circle Midnight, and I was afraid to hope!" She thrust out her hand, dimpling. "I'm Dani Abforth."

Thea felt her heart lighten. The girl's laughter was infectious. "Thea Harman. Unity." It was the age-old greeting of the witches, the symbol of their harmony, their oneness.

"Unity," Dani murmured. Then her eyes widened. "Harman? You're a Hearth-Woman? A daughter of Hellewise? Really?"

Thea laughed. "We're all daughters of Hellewise."

"Yes, but—you know what I mean. You're a direct descendent. I'm honored."

"Well, I'm honored, too. Abforth is 'All-bringing-forth,' isn't it? That's a pretty impressive line itself." Dani was still looking awed, so Thea said quickly, "My cousin's here, too—Blaise Harman. We're both new—but you must be, too. I've never seen you around Vegas before."

"We moved in last month, just in time to start school," Dani said. Her brow puckered. "But if *you're* new, what do you mean you haven't seen me around?"

Thea sighed. "Well, it's kind of complicated. . . ."

A bell rang. Both she and Dani looked at the school building in frustration, then at each other.

"Meet me here at lunch?" Dani asked.

Thea nodded, asked which way her French class was, and then flew off toward the other side of the building.

She sat through her next two classes trying to actually listen to the teachers. She didn't know what else to do. She had to concentrate to keep the image of gray-flecked green eyes out of her mind.

At lunch, she found Dani sitting on the steps out front. Thea settled beside her and opened a bottle of Evian water and a chocolate yogurt she'd bought at the snack bar.

"You were going to explain how you know Vegas," Dani said. She spoke softly because there were kids everywhere in the front courtyard, sprawled in the sun with paper bags.

Thea eyed a row of sago palms and felt herself

sighing again. "Blaise and I—our mothers died when we were born. They were twin sisters. And then both our *dads* died. So we grew up sort of moving around from relative to relative. We usually spend the summers with Grandma Harman, and we live with somebody else during the school year. But these last couple of years . . . well, we've been in five high schools since we were sophomores."

"*Five?*"

"Five. I think five. Isis knows, it could be six."

"But *why?*"

"We keep getting expelled," Thea said succinctly.

"But—"

"It's Blaise's fault," Thea said. She was mad at Blaise. "She does—*things*—to boys. Human boys. And somehow it always ends up getting us kicked out of school. Both of us, because I'm always too stupid to tell them she's the one responsible."

"Not stupid, I bet. Loyal," Dani said warmly, and put her hand on Thea's. Thea squeezed it, taking some comfort in the sympathy.

"Anyway, this year we were in New Hampshire living with our Uncle Galen—and Blaise did it again. To the captain of the football team. His name was Randy Marik. . . ."

When Thea stopped, Dani said, "What happened to him?"

"He burned the school down for her."

Dani made a sound halfway between a snort and a giggle. Then she straightened out her face quickly. "Sorry, not funny. *For* her?"

Thea leaned against the wrought-iron stair railing.

"That's what Blaise likes," she said bleakly. "Having power over guys, messing with their minds. Getting them to do things they would never ordinarily do. To prove their love, you know. But the thing is, she's never satisfied until they're completely destroyed. . . ." She shook her head. "You should have seen Randy at the end. He'd lost his mind. I don't think he'll ever get it back."

Dani wasn't smiling anymore. "Power like that . . . she sounds like Aphrodite," she said softly.

And that's right, Thea thought. Aphrodite, the Greek goddess of love who could turn passion into a weapon that brought the whole world to its knees.

"Remind me sometime to tell you what she's done to the other guys she's played. In a way, Randy was lucky. . . ."

Thea took a breath. "So, anyway, we got shipped back here to Grandma Harman because there weren't any other relatives willing to take us. They figured if Gran couldn't straighten us up, nobody could."

"But that must be *wonderful*," Dani said. "I mean, living with *the* Crone. Part of the reason my mom moved us here was that she wanted to study with your grandmother."

Thea nodded. "Yeah, people come from all over to take her classes, or to buy her amulets and things. She's not always easy to live with, though," Thea added wryly. "She goes through a couple of apprentices a year."

"So is she going to straighten Blaise up?"

"I don't think *anybody* can. What Blaise does—it's just her nature, the way it's a cat's nature to play with mice. And if we get in trouble again, Gran says she's going to send us to our aunt Ursula at the Connecticut enclave."

"The Convent?"

"Yeah."

"Then you'd better stay out of trouble."

"I *know*. Dani, what's this school like? I mean, is it the kind of place where Blaise *can* keep out of trouble?"

"Well . . ." Dani looked dismayed. "Well—I told you before, there's only two other witches in our class, and they're both Circle Midnight. Maybe you know them . . . Vivienne Morrigan and Selene Lucna?"

Thea's heart sank. Vivienne and Selene—she'd seen them going to summer Circles, wearing the darkest robes of any of the Circle Midnight girls. The two of them plus Blaise would make . . . well, a lethal combination.

"Maybe if you explain to them how important it is, they might help you keep Blaise under control," Dani said. "You want to go talk to them now? They'll be on the patio by the cafeteria—I usually eat with them there."

"Um . . ." Thea hesitated. Talking to those two— well, she doubted it would help. But on the other hand, she didn't have a better idea. "Why not?"

On the way to the cafeteria, she saw something that made her stop dead. Taped to the stucco wall was a giant piece of butcher paper, painted orange and black at the margins. In the center was a grotesque figure: an old woman with a black dress, disheveled white hair, and a wart-covered, haglike face. She was straddling a broom and wearing a pointy hat. Lettering under the picture said COMING OCTOBER 31 . . . THE ULTIMATE HALLOWEEN PARTY.

Hands on hips, Thea said, *"When* will they learn that witches never wore pointy hats?"

Dani snorted, her heart-shaped face surprisingly dangerous. "You know, maybe your cousin has the right idea after all."

Thea looked at her, startled.

"Well, they *are* an inferior species. You have to admit that. And maybe it sounds prejudiced, but then they're so prejudiced themselves." She leaned closer to Thea. "You know, they even have prejudices against *skin.*"

She held out her arm. Thea looked at the flawless skin, which was a deep, clear brown. "They'd think *we* were two different races," Dani said, pressing her arm against Thea's tan one. "And that maybe one was better than the other one."

Thea couldn't deny it. All she could say, feebly, was, "Well, two wrongs don't make a right. . . ."

"But three lefts do!" Dani burst out, finishing the old witch carol. Then she dissolved into laughter and led Thea to the patio.

"Let's see, they should be over there. . . . Oh. Oops."

Oops, Thea thought.

Vivienne and Selene were at a secluded table on the far side. Blaise was with them.

"I should have known she'd find them first thing," Thea muttered. From the way the three girls had their heads together, it looked as if trouble were brewing already.

As Thea and Dani approached the table, Blaise looked up. "Where've you been?" she said, waving a finger reproachfully. "I've been waiting to introduce you."

Everybody said hello. Then Thea sat down and studied the other two girls.

Vivienne had fox-red hair and looked tall even sitting down. Her face was animated; she seemed sparkling with energy. Selene was a platinum blond with sleepy blue eyes. She was smaller, and moved with languid grace.

Now, how do I politely say, "Please help me suppress my cousin?" Thea wondered. She could already tell it wouldn't be much use. Viv and Selene seemed to be under Blaise's spell already—they turned to her every other second as if checking for approval. Even Dani was watching Blaise with something like fascinated awe.

Blaise had that effect on people.

"So we were just talking about guys," Selene said, twirling a straw languorously in her bottle of Snapple iced tea. Thea's heart plummeted.

"Toyboys," Vivienne clarified in a lovely melodious voice. Thea felt the beginnings of a bad headache.

No wonder Blaise is smirking, she thought. These girls are *just like her*. She'd seen it at other schools: young witches who seemed to flirt with breaking Night World law by flaunting inhuman power over boys.

"Aren't there any of *our* kind of guys here?" Thea asked, as a last hope.

Vivienne rolled her eyes. "One sophomore. Alaric Breedlove, Circle Twilight. That's *it*. This place is a desert—no pun intended."

Thea wasn't really surprised. There were always more witch girls than guys—and nobody seemed to know why. More girls got born, more survived to grow up. And in some places the ratio was particularly unbalanced.

"So we just have to make do," Selene drawled. "But that can be fun sometimes. Homecoming dance is this Saturday, and I've got my boy all picked out."

"So," Blaise said, "have I." She glanced at Thea significantly.

And there it was. Thea felt her throat close.

"Eric Ross," Blaise said, savoring the words. "And Viv and Sel have told me *allll* about him."

"Eric?" Dani said. "He's the basketball star, isn't he?"

"And the baseball star," Vivienne said in her beautiful voice. "And the tennis star. And he's smart—he takes honors courses and works at the animal hospital, too. He's studying to get into U.C. Davis. To be a vet, you know."

So that's why he cared about the snake, Thea thought. And why he's got flatworms in his notebook.

"And he's so cute," Selene murmured. "He's so shy with girls—he can hardly talk around them. None of us have gotten anywhere with him."

"That's because you used the wrong methods," Blaise said, and her eyes were very smoky.

Thea's insides seemed hollow and there was a circlet of pain around her head. She did the only thing she could think of.

"Blaise," she said. She looked her cousin directly in the face, making an open appeal. "Blaise, listen. I hardly ever ask anything of you, right? But now I'm asking something. I want you to leave Eric alone. Can you do that—for me? For the sake of Unity?"

Blaise blinked slowly. She took a long drink of iced tea. "Why, Thea, you're getting all worked up."

"I am *not*."

"I didn't know you cared."

"I *don't*. I mean—of course I don't care about *him*. But I'm worried about you, about all of us. I think . . ." Thea hadn't meant to say this, but she found the words spilling out anyway. "I think he might have some suspicions about us. This morning he told me that I seemed so different from other girls. . . ." She managed to stop herself before she mentioned that he'd guessed she had healed him. *That* would be incredibly dangerous, especially since she didn't know who Vivienne or Selene might blab to.

Blaise's pupils were large. "You mean—you think he's a psychic?"

"No, no." She knew he *wasn't* a psychic. She'd been inside his mind, and he wasn't from any lost witch family. He didn't have any powers. He was as much a human as that snake had been a snake.

"Well, then," Blaise said. She chuckled, a rich, rippling sound. "He just thinks you're different—and *that's* hardly something to worry about. We *want* them to think we're different."

She didn't understand. And Thea couldn't explain. Not without getting herself into very hot water.

"So, if you don't mind, we'll just consider my claim staked," Blaise said courteously. "Now, let's see, what to do with the boys at the dance. First, I think we need to spill their blood."

"Spill *what?*" Dani said, sitting up.

"Just a little blood," Blaise told her absently. "It's going to be absolutely vital for some of the spells we'll want to do later."

"Well, good luck," Dani said. "Humans don't like blood—they're going to run like bunnies from you after that."

Blaise regarded her with a half-smile. "I don't think so," she said. "You don't understand this business yet. If it's done right, they don't run. They're scared; they're shocked; and they just keep coming back for more."

Dani looked shocked herself—and still fascinated. "But why do you want to hurt them?"

"We're just doing what comes naturally," Blaise purred.

I don't care Thea thought, it's none of my business.

She heard herself say, "No."

She was staring at a pile of squashed napkins in her hand. Out of the corner of her eye she could see

Blaise's exasperated expression. The others might not know what Thea was saying no *to*, but Blaise always understood her cousin.

"I asked you before if you wanted him," Blaise said. "And you said you didn't. So now you're changing your mind? You're going to play him?"

Thea stared at her wad of napkins. What could she say? I can't because I'm scared? I can't because something happened between him and me this morning and I don't know what it was? I can't because if I keep seeing him I have this feeling I might break the law, and I don't mean the one about never telling humans that we exist; I mean the other one, the one about never falling in love. . . .

Don't be *ridiculous*.

That sort of thing is out of the question, she told herself. All you want is to keep him from ending up like Randy Marik. And you can do *that* without getting involved.

"I'm saying I want him," she said out loud.

"You're going to play him?"

"I'm going to play him."

"Well." Instead of snarling, Blaise laughed. "Well, congratulations. My little cousin is growing up at last."

"Oh, please." Thea gave her a look. She and Blaise had been born on two different days—just barely. Blaise had been born one minute before midnight, and Thea one minute after. It was another reason they were so connected—but Thea hated it when Blaise acted older.

Blaise just smiled, her gray eyes glinting. "And,

look—there's lover boy right now," she said, feigning elaborate surprise. Thea followed her nod and saw a figure with sandy hair and long legs at the other side of the patio.

"What luck," Blaise said. "Why don't you just walk over and ask him to the dance?"

CHAPTER
4

At that moment Thea almost hated her cousin.

But there was no choice. Four pairs of eyes were watching her: Blaise's gray eyes, Vivienne's emerald green, Selene's clear blue, and Dani's velvety dark ones. They were waiting.

Thea got up and began the long walk across the patio.

She felt as if *everyone* was watching her. She tried to keep her steps measured and confident, her face serene. It wasn't easy. The closer she got to that sandy hair, the more she wanted to turn and run. She had tunnel vision now: everything on the sides was a blur; the only clear thing was Eric's profile.

Just as she got within earshot, he glanced up and saw her coming.

He looked startled. For a moment his eyes met hers: a deeper green than Vivienne's, more intense and more innocent.

Then, without a word, he turned away and walked quickly down a path between two buildings. He was gone before Thea knew what was happening.

She stood rooted to the ground. There was a huge amount of empty space inside her, with only her uncomfortably pounding heart trying to fill it.

Okay; he hates me. I don't blame him. Maybe it's good; maybe Blaise will say we can all forget him now.

But when she went back to the shady table, Blaise was frowning thoughtfully.

"You just don't have the technique yet," she said. "Never mind. I can coach you."

"Viv and I can help, too," Selene murmured. "You'll learn fast."

"*No*—thank you," Thea said. Her pride was hurt and her cheeks were on fire. "I can do it myself. Tomorrow. I have a plan already."

Dani squeezed her hand under the table. "You'll do fine."

Blaise said, "Just make sure it's tomorrow. Or I might think you don't really want him."

And then, to Thea's immense relief, the bell rang.

"Hawthorne, yarrow, angelica . . ." Thea peered through the thick blue glass of an unlabeled jar. "Some kind of nasty powder . . ."

She was in the front room of her grandmother's shop, deserted now because it was closed for the evening. Just being with all these herbs and gems and amulets gave her a feeling of comfort. Of control.

I love this place, she thought, looking around at

the floor-to-ceiling shelves of bottles and boxes and dusty vials. One whole wall was devoted to trays of stones—unpolished and polished, rare and semiprecious, some with symbols or words of power engraved on them, some dirty and fresh from the earth. Thea liked putting her hands in them and murmuring their names: tourmaline, amethyst, honey topaz, white jade.

And then there were the good-smelling herbs: everything you needed to cure indigestion or to call a lover; to soothe arthritis or to curse your landlord. Some of these—the simples—worked whether you were a witch or not. They were just natural remedies, and Gran even sold them to humans. But the *real* spells required both arcane knowledge and psychic power, and no human could make them active.

Thea was whipping up a real spell.

First, heartsease. That was good for any love charm. Thea opened a canister and fingered the dried purple and yellow flowers gently. Then she dropped a handful of them into a fine mesh bag.

What else? Rose petals were a given. She unstopped a large ceramic jar and got a whiff of sweetness as she sprinkled them in.

Chamomile, yes. Rosemary, yes. Lavender . . . she twisted the cork out of a small vial of lavender essence. She could use some of *that* right this minute. She mixed it in her palm with a teaspoon of jojoba oil, then dabbed the fragrant liquid on her temples and at the back of her neck.

Blood, flow! Headache, go!

The tension in her neck started to ease almost instantly. She took a long breath and looked around.

Some bones of the earth would help. Rose quartz carved in the shape of a heart for attraction. A lump of raw amber for charm. Oh, and throw in a lodestone for magnetism and a couple of small garnets for fire.

It was done. Tomorrow morning she'd take a bath, letting this giant tea bag infuse the water while she burned a circle of red candles. She'd soak in the potent mixture, letting the smell of it, the essence of it, seep into her skin. And when she got out, she'd be irresistible.

She was about to walk away when a leather pouch caught her eye.

No. Not *that*, she told herself. You've got a mixture here to promote interest and affection. It's plenty strong enough just to get him to listen to you.

You don't *want* anything stronger.

But she found herself picking up the soft pouch anyway. Opening it, just to look inside.

It was full of reddish-brown chips, each about the size of a thumbnail with a woody, aromatic smell.

Yemonja root. Guaranteed to draw an unwilling heart. But usually forbidden to maidens.

Recklessly, not letting herself think about it, Thea transferred half a dozen chips to her mesh bag. Then she put the worn leather pouch back on its shelf.

"Figured it out yet?" a voice behind her said.

Thea whirled. Gran was standing at the foot of the narrow stairway that led to the apartment above the store.

"Uh—what?" She held the mesh bag behind her back.

"Your specialty. Herbs, stones, amulets . . . I hope you're not going to be one of those chanting girls. I hate that whiny music."

Thea loved the music. In fact, she loved all the things Gran had mentioned—but she loved animals even better. And there wasn't much of a place for animals in witch life, not since familiars had been outlawed during the Burning Times.

You could use *bits* of animals, sure. Lizard foot and nightingale tongue. Blaise was always trying to get hold of Thea's animals for just that purpose, and Thea was always fighting her off.

"I don't know, Gran," she said. "I'm still thinking."

"Well, you've got time—but not too *much*," her grandmother said, walking slowly toward her. Edgith Harman's face was a mass of creases, she hunched, and she used two canes—but that wasn't bad for a woman over a hundred who ran her own business and tyrannized every witch in the country.

"Remember, you've got some decisions to make when you hit eighteen. You and Blaise are the last of our line. The last two direct descendants of Hellewise. That means you have a responsibility—you have to set an example."

"I know." At eighteen, she would have to decide not just her specialty, but which Circle she would join for life: Twilight or Midnight. "I'll think about it, Gran," she promised, putting her free arm around the old woman. "I've still got six months."

Gran stroked Thea's hair with a veined, gentle hand. It chased the last of Thea's headache away. Still holding the mesh bag behind her back, she said, "Gran? Are you really mad about having us here for the school year?"

"Well, you eat too much and you leave hair in the shower . . . but I guess I can stand it." Gran smiled, then frowned. "Just as long as you stay in line until the end of the month."

There it was again. "But what's happening at the end of the month?"

Gran gave her a look. "Samhain, of course! All Hallow's Eve."

"I know *that*," Thea said. Even the humans celebrated Halloween. She wondered if Gran was having one of her vague spells.

"Samhain—and the Inner Circle," Gran said abruptly. "They've picked the desert for their ceremony this year."

"The desert—you mean *here?* The Inner Circle is coming *here?* Mother Cybele and Aradia and all of them?"

"All of them," Gran said. Suddenly her wrinkles looked grim. "And by Air and Fire, I'm not having them come here just to see you girls screw up. I have a reputation, you know."

Thea nodded a little dazedly. "I—well, no wonder you were worried. We won't embarrass you. I promise."

"Good."

As Thea discreetly tucked the mesh bag under her arm and started for the stairs, the old woman added,

"You'd better toss some plantain into that mix to bind it all together."

Thea felt herself blushing furiously. "Uh . . . thanks, Gran," she said, and went to look for plantain.

Above the shop were two tiny bedrooms and a kitchenette. Grandma had one bedroom and Thea and Blaise shared the other. Tobias, Gran's apprentice, had been bumped to the workshop downstairs.

Blaise was lying on her bed, reading a thick book with a red cover. Poetry. Despite her frivolous act, she wasn't stupid.

"Guess what," Thea said, and without waiting for Blaise to guess, told her about the Inner Circle coming.

She watched to see if the news would scare Blaise—or at least alarm her into good intentions. But Blaise just yawned and stretched like a well-fed cat.

"Good. Maybe we can watch how they summon the ancestors again." She raised her eyebrows at Thea meaningfully. Two years ago in Vermont, while the human world was trick-or-treating, they'd hidden behind maple trees and spied on the Samhain summoning. They'd seen the elders use the magic of Hecate, the most ancient witch of all, the goddess of moon and night and sorcery, to bring spirits across the veil. For Thea it had been scary but exciting, for Blaise just exciting.

Thea gave up on trying to alarm Blaise.

*   *   *

Thea looked at the three star-shaped blue flowers lying on her palm. Then, one by one, she ate them.

"Now say *'Ego borago guadia semper ago,'* " Selene instructed. "It means, 'I, borage, always bring courage.' Old Roman spell."

Thea muttered the words. For the second day in a row, she was on the patio looking at a sandy head across the room.

"Go get 'im, tiger," Blaise said. Vivienne and Dani nodded encouragingly. Thea squared her shoulders and started across the room.

As soon as Eric saw her coming he went down the side path.

You *idiot*, Thea thought. You don't know what's good for you. Maybe I should just let Blaise have you.

But she followed him. He was standing just beyond the buildings, staring into the distance. She could only see his profile, which was nice—clean and somehow lonely.

Thea swallowed, tasting a lingering sweetness from the borage flowers. What to say? She wasn't used to talking to humans—especially human boys.

I'll just say "What's up?" and be casual, she thought. But when she opened her mouth, what came out was, "I'm sorry."

He turned immediately. He looked startled. "You're sorry?"

"Yes. I'm sorry I was so mean. What do you think I was following you for?"

Eric blinked—and Thea thought his cheeks colored under his tan. "I thought you were mad because I kept staring at you. I was trying not to get you madder."

"You were staring at me?" Thea felt a little flushed herself. As if the herbs from her bath were steaming fragrantly out of her skin.

"Well—I kept trying not to. I think I've got it down to one look every thirty seconds now." He said it seriously.

Thea wanted to laugh. "It's okay. I don't mind," she said. Yes, she could definitely smell the love potion now. The heady floral scent of rose and heartsease, plus the spice of yemonja root.

Eric seemed to take her at her word. He was definitely staring. *"I'm* sorry I acted like such a jerk before. With the snake, I mean. I really wasn't trying to feed you a line."

Alarm whispered through Thea. She didn't want to think about what had happened in the desert.

"Yes, okay, I know," she said. He was watching her so intently, his eyes such a deep green. "Well—you see, the reason I wanted to talk to you was . . . you know, there's the Homecoming dance this Saturday. So I thought we could maybe go together."

She remembered at the last instant that in human society boys frequently asked girls to dances. Maybe she'd been too direct.

But he looked—well, extremely pleased. "You're kidding! You're serious? You'd go with me?"

Thea just nodded.

"But that's terrific. I mean—*thanks.*" He was as excited as a kid at Beltane. Then his face clouded over.

"I forgot, though. I promised Dr. Salinger—that's my boss at the pet hospital—that I'd spend the night there Saturday. Midnight to eight A.M. Somebody needs to watch the animals that stay overnight, and Dr. Salinger's going to a conference out of town."

"It doesn't matter," Thea said. "We'll just go to the dance before midnight." She was relieved. It meant less time play-acting in front of Blaise.

"It's a date, then." He still looked so happy. "And, Thea?" He said the name shyly, as if almost afraid to use it. "Maybe—maybe we could do something else sometime. I mean, we could go out, or you could come over to my house. . . ."

"Uh . . ." The yemonja smell was *really* making her dizzy. "Uh . . . well, this week—I'm trying to get adjusted to the new school and all. But maybe later."

"Okay. Later." His smile was unexpected, astonishing. It transformed his face, turning the sweet, serious shyness into charismatic radiance. "If there's any way I can help, just ask."

Why, he's handsome, Thea thought. She felt a sort of tug at her insides, like a bird being charmed out of a tree. She hadn't realized how attractive he was, or how the gray flecks in his eyes seemed to catch sunlight. . . .

Stop that! she told herself abruptly. This is *business*, and he's *vermin*. She felt a flush of shame at using the word, even in thought. But she had to do something. Without meaning to, she'd moved closer to him, so she was looking up into his face. Now they were only inches apart and she was feeling distinctly giddy.

"I have to go—*now*. I'll see you later," she murmured, and made herself back up.

"Later," he said. He was still glowing.

Thea fled.

Wednesday, Thursday, and Friday, she tried to ignore him. Avoided him in the halls, acting as busy as possible. He seemed to understand, and didn't chase her down. She just wished he wouldn't look so dreamy and *happy* all the time.

And then there was Blaise. Blaise already had a couple of husky football players who followed her everywhere, Buck and Duane—but neither of them was invited to the dance. Blaise had a unique method of choosing a partner. She told them all to go away.

"You don't want me," she said to a gorgeous Asian-American guy with one earring.

It was lunch break on Thursday, and the witches had a whole table to themselves: Vivienne and Selene with Blaise on one side; Dani with Thea on the other. The gorgeous guy had one knee on a chair and was looking very nervous.

"You can't afford me, Kevin. I'll ruin you. Better get out of here," Blaise said, all the while looking up with sleeping fire in her gray eyes.

Kevin shifted. "But I'm rich." He said it simply, without affectation.

"I'm not talking about money," Blaise said. She gave a deprecating smile. "And anyway, I don't think you're really interested."

"Are you kidding? I'm crazy about you. Every time I see you . . . I don't know; it just makes me crazy."

He glanced at the other girls and Thea knew he was uncomfortable at having an audience. But not uncomfortable enough to stop talking. "I'd do anything for you."

"No, I don't think so." Blaise was toying with a ring on her left index finger.

"What's that?" Vivienne interjected nonchalantly.

"Hm? Oh, just a little diamond," Blaise said. She held out her hand and light scintillated. "Stuart Mac-Ready gave it to me this morning."

Kevin shifted again. "I can buy you dozens of rings."

Thea felt sorry for him. He seemed like an okay guy, and she'd heard him talk about wanting to be a musician. But she knew from long experience that it wouldn't do any good to tell him to get out of here. It would only make him more stubborn.

"But I wouldn't want a ring from you," Blaise was saying in a soft, chiding voice. "Stuart gave this to me because it was the only memento he had of his mom. It meant everything to him—so he wanted me to have it."

"I'd do the same thing," Kevin said.

Blaise just shook her head. "I don't think so."

"Yes, I would."

"No. The thing that means the most to you is your car, and you'd never give that up."

Thea had seen the car. It was a silver-gray Porsche. Kevin lovingly touched it up with a chamois in the school parking lot every morning.

Now Kevin looked confused. "But—that car's not

really mine. It belongs to my parents. They just let me use it."

Blaise nodded understandingly. "You see? I told you you wouldn't. Now, why don't you go away like a good boy?"

Kevin seemed to collapse internally. He stared at Blaise pleadingly, not making a move to go away. At last, Blaise tilted her head at the football flunkies.

"C'mon, man," one flunky—Thea thought it was Duane—said. They took Kevin by the shoulders and propelled him away. Kevin kept looking back.

Blaise dusted her fingers off briskly.

Selene pushed back pale hair and drawled, "Think he'll cough up the car?"

"Well . . ." Blaise smiled. "Let's just say I think I'll have transportation to the dance. Of course, I'm still not sure who I'm taking. . . ."

Thea got up. Dani had sat silently through lunch, and now she was watching Blaise, her velvety dark eyes half horrified and half admiring.

"I'm getting out of here," Thea said significantly, and was relieved when Dani stopped staring at Blaise and stood up.

"Oh, by the way," Blaise said, picking up her backpack, "I forgot to give you this." She handed Thea a small vial, the size that perfume samples came in.

"What's it for?"

"For the dance. You know, to put the boys' blood in."

CHAPTER

5

What?'' Thea said. This was something she *could* speak out about. "Blaise, are you out of your mind?"

"I hope you're not saying you don't want to do spells," Blaise said dangerously. "That's part of it, you know."

"I'm saying there's no way we can get enough blood to fill *this* without them noticing. What are we going to tell them? 'I just want a little to remember you by?' "

"Use your ingenuity," Vivienne said musically, twining a red-gold strand of hair around her fingers.

"In a pinch we could always use the Cup of Lethe," Blaise added calmly. "Then no matter what we do, they won't remember."

Thea nearly fell over. What Blaise was suggesting was like using a nuclear bomb to swat a fly. "You *are* crazy," she said quietly. "You know that maidens aren't allowed to use that kind of spell, and we probably won't even be able to use it when we're mothers, and probably not even when we're *crones*. That's stuff for the *elders*.'' She stared at Blaise until the gray eyes dropped.

"I don't believe in classifying some spells as forbidden," Blaise said loftily, but she didn't look back at Thea and she didn't pursue the subject.

As she and Dani left the patio, Thea noticed that Dani had taken one of the small vials.

"Are you going to the dance?"

"I guess so." Dani shrugged lithe shoulders. "John Finkelstein from our world lit class asked me a couple weeks ago. I've never been to one of *their* dances before—but maybe this is the time to start."

Now what did *that* mean? Thea felt uneasy. "And you're planning to put a spell on him?"

"You mean this?" She twisted the vial in her fingers. "I don't know. I figured I'd take it just in case. . . ." She looked up at Thea defensively. "You took one for Eric."

Thea hesitated. She hadn't talked to Dani about Eric yet. Part of her wanted to and part of her was scared. What did Dani really think of Outsiders, anyway?

"After all," Dani said, her sweet face tranquil, "they're only humans."

Saturday night Thea took a dress out of the closet. It was pale green—so pale that it almost looked white—and designed along Grecian lines. Witch clothes had to feel good as well as look good, and

this dress was soft and lightweight, swirling beautifully when she turned.

Blaise wasn't wearing a dress. She was wearing a
tuxedo. It had a red silk bow tie and cummerbund
and it looked fantastic on her.

This is probably going to be the only dance in history where the most popular girl has on cufflinks,
Thea thought.

Eric arrived right on time. He knocked at the front
door of the shop, the door that only Outsiders used.
Night People came around back, to a door that was
unmarked except for what looked like a bit of graf-
fiti—a spray-painted black dahlia.

Okay, Thea thought. She took a deep breath before
she unlocked the door and let him in.

This is business, business, business. . . .

But the first moment wasn't as awkward as she'd
feared. He smiled and held out a corsage of white
orchids. She smiled and took it. Then she said, "You
look nice."

His suit was pale fatigue brown, loose and comfortable looking. "Me? *You* look nice. I mean—you look
wonderful. That color makes your hair look just like
gold." Then he glanced down at himself apologeti-
cally. "I don't go to many dances, I'm afraid."

"Don't you?" She'd heard girls talking about him
at school. It seemed as if everyone liked him, wanted
to get close to him.

"No, I'm usually pretty busy. You know, working,
playing sports." He added more softly, "And I have
a hard time thinking of things to say around girls."

Funny, you never seem to have a problem around

me, Thea thought. She saw him looking the shop over.

"It's my grandmother's store. She sells all kinds of things here, from all around the world." She watched him closely. This was an important test. If he—a human—believed in this stuff, he was either a New Age geek or dangerously close to the truth.

"It's cool," he said, and she was happy to see that he was lying. "I mean," he said, obviously struggling to find a polite way to praise the voodoo dolls and wand crystals, "I think people can really affect their bodies by changing their state of mind."

You don't know how right you are, Thea thought.

There was a clack of high heels on wood, and Blaise came down the stairs. Her shoes appeared first, then her fitted trouser legs, then all the curves, emphasized here and there with brilliant red silk. Finally came her shoulders and head, her midnight hair half up and half down, framing her face in stormy dark curls.

Thea glanced sideways at Eric.

He was smiling at Blaise, but not in the goofy, dying-sheep way other guys smiled. His was just a genuine grin.

"Hi, Blaise," he said. "Going to the dance? We can take you if you need a lift."

Blaise stopped dead. Then she gave him a blistering glare. "Thank you, I have my own date. I'm just going to pick him up now."

On the way to the door, she looked hard at Thea. "You do have everything you need for tonight—don't you?"

The vial was in Thea's pale green clutch purse. Thea still didn't know how she could possibly get it filled, but she nodded tightly.

"Good." Blaise swept out and got into a silver-gray Porsche that was parked at the curb. Kevin's car. But, as Thea knew, she wasn't going to pick up Kevin.

"I think I made her mad," Eric said.

"Don't worry. Blaise likes being mad. Should we go now?"

Business, business, business, Thea chanted to herself as they walked into the school cafeteria. It had been completely transformed from its daytime identity. The lights and music were oddly thrilling and the whirl of color out on the dance floor was strangely inviting.

I'm not here to have fun, Thea told herself again. But her blood seemed to be sparkling. She saw Eric glance at her conspiratorially and she could almost feel what he was feeling—as if they were two kids standing hand in hand at the edge of some incredible carnival.

"Uh, I should tell you," Eric said. "I can't really dance—except for slow ones."

Oh, great. But of course this was what she was here to do. To put on a show of romancing Eric for Blaise.

A slow song was starting that minute. Thea shut her eyes briefly and resigned herself to fate—which didn't seem all *that* awful as she and Eric stepped out onto the floor.

Terpsichore, Muse of the Dance, help me not make

a fool of myself. She'd never been so close to a human boy, and she'd never tried to dance to human music. But Eric didn't seem to notice her lack of experience.

"You know, I can't believe this," he said. His arms were around her lightly, almost reverently. As if he were afraid she'd break if he held her too hard.

"What can't you believe?"

"Well . . ." He shook his head. "Everything, I guess. That I'm here with you. And that it all feels so easy. And that you always *smell* so good."

Thea laughed in spite of herself. "I didn't use any yemonja this time—" she began, and then she almost bit her tongue. Adrenaline washed over her in a wave of painful tingles.

Was she crazy? She was blurting out *spell ingredients*, for Earth's sake. He was too easy to talk to, that was the problem. Every so often she'd forget he wasn't a witch.

"You okay?" he said as her silence stretched on. His voice was concerned.

No, I am not okay. I've got Blaise on one side and the laws of the Night World on the other, and they're both out to get me. And I don't even know if you're worth it. . . .

"Can I ask you something?" she said abruptly. "Why did you knock me out of the way of that snake?"

"Huh? It was in a striking coil. You could have got bit."

"But so could you." So *did* you.

He frowned as if stricken by one of those unsolvable mysteries of life. "Yeah . . . but that didn't seem so bad somehow. I suppose that sounds stupid."

Thea didn't know how to answer. And she was suddenly in terrible conflict about what to do. Her body seemed to want her to lean her head against Eric's shoulder, but her mind was yelling in alarm at the very thought.

At that moment she heard loud voices at the edge of the dance floor.

"Get out of the way," a guy in a blue jacket was saying. "She smiled at me, and I'm going over there."

"It was *me* she was smiling at, you jerk," a guy in a gray jacket snapped back. "So just back off and let me go."

Expletives. "It was *me*, and you'd better get out of the way."

More expletives. "It was *me*, and you'd better let go."

A fistfight started. Chaperones came running.

Guess who's here? Thea asked herself. She had no trouble at all locating Blaise. The red-trimmed tuxedo was surrounded by a ring of guys, which was surrounded by a ring of abandoned and angry girls.

"Maybe we should go over and say hi," Thea said. She wanted to warn Blaise about starting a riot.

"Okay. She sure is popular, isn't she?"

They managed to worm their way through the encircling crowd. Blaise was in her element, glorying in the adulation and confusion.

"I waited for an hour and a half, but you never showed up," a very pale Kevin was saying to her. He was wearing an immaculate white silk shirt and exquisitely tailored black pants. His eyes were hollow.

"Maybe you gave me the wrong address," Blaise said thoughtfully. "I couldn't find your house." She had her hand tucked into the arm of a very tall guy with shoulder-length blond hair, who looked as if he worked out four or five hours a day. "Anyway, you want to dance?"

Kevin looked at the blond guy, who looked back impassively, his cleft chin rock hard.

"Don't mind Sergio," Blaise said. "He was just keeping me company. Do you *not* want to dance?"

Kevin's eyes fell. "Well, yeah, of course I want to. . . ."

As Blaise detached herself from Sergio, Thea leaned forward. "You'd better not do anything too public," she hissed in her cousin's ear. "There's already been one fight."

Blaise just gave her an amused glance and took Kevin's arm. Most of the boys followed her, and with the crowd gone, Thea saw Dani at a small table. She was wearing a sparkling gold dress and she was alone.

"Let's go sit," Eric said, before Thea could even get a word out. She threw him a grateful look.

"Where's John?" Thea asked as they pulled chairs to the table.

Dani nodded toward the pack following Blaise.

"I don't mind, though," she said, sipping a cup of punch philosophically. "He was kind of boring. I don't know about all this dance stuff."

Thea knew she meant it was different from Circle

dances, where everyone was in harmony and there was no pairing off. You danced with the elements and with everybody else, all one big interconnected whole.

Eric volunteered to get more punch.

"How's it going with him?" Dani asked in a low voice when he was gone. Her velvety dark eyes searched Thea's curiously.

"Everything's okay so far," Thea said evasively. Then she looked out toward the dance floor. "I see Viv and Selene are here."

"Yeah. I think Vivienne already got her blood. She stabbed Tyrone with her corsage pin."

"How clever," Thea said. Vivienne was wearing a black dress that made her hair look like flame, and Selene was in deep violet that showed off her blondness. They both seemed to be having a wonderful time.

Dani yawned. "I think I'll probably go home early—" she began, and then she broke off.

Some kind of a disturbance had begun on the other side of the room, in front of the main entrance. People were scuffling. At first, Thea thought it was just another minor fracas over Blaise—but then a figure came staggering out under the lights of the dance floor.

"I want to *know*," the voice said in dissonant tones that rose over the music. "I want to *knoooow*."

The band stopped. People turned. Something about the voice made them do that. It was so obviously abnormal, the cadence wrong even for somebody who was drunk. This was someone who was *disturbed*.

Thea stood up.

"I want to *knoooow,*" the figure said again, sounding lost and petulant. Then it turned and Thea felt ice down her spine.

The person was wearing a Halloween mask.

A kid's plastic mask of a football player, the kind held on with an elastic string. Perfectly appropriate for a Halloween dance. But at Homecoming, it was grotesque.

Oh, Eileithyia, Thea thought.

"Can you *tell* me?" the figure asked a short girl in black ruffles. She backed away, reaching for her dance partner.

Mr. Adkins, Thea's physics teacher, came jogging up, his tie fluttering. None of the other chaperones seemed to be around—probably because they were out somewhere trying to control fights over Blaise, Thea thought.

"Okay, let's settle; settle," Mr. Adkins said, making motions as if the figure were an unruly class. "Let's just take it easy. . . ."

The guy in the Halloween mask pulled something out of his jacket. It glinted like a rainbow under the colored dance floor lights, reflective as a mirror.

"A straight razor," Dani said in a hushed voice. "Queen Isis, where'd he get that?"

Something about the weapon—maybe the fact that it was so weird, so old-fashioned—made it scarier than a knife. Thea pictured the way even a safety razor could slice flesh.

Mr. Adkins was backing away, arms held out as if

to protect the students behind him. His eyes were frightened.

I have to stop this, Thea thought. The problem was that she had no idea how. If it had been an animal, she could have stepped out and tried mind control. But she couldn't control a person.

She started walking anyway, slowly, so as not to attract attention. She skirted the edge of the crowd around the dance floor until she drew parallel with the masked guy.

Who by now had switched to a new question. "Have you *seen* her?" he said. He kept asking it as he walked, and people kept backing away. Vivienne and Selene drew to either side with their dates. The razor glittered.

Thea looked toward the opposite end of the dance floor, where Blaise was standing with Kevin Imamura.

With no Buck, no Duane to protect her. But Blaise didn't look frightened. That was one thing about Blaise—she had magnificent physical courage. She was standing with one hand on her hip and Thea could tell that she knew exactly who was coming her way.

In between moving couples, Thea glimpsed something else. Eric was on the other side of the dance floor, holding two cups of punch in one hand and one in the other. He was keeping pace with the masked guy, just as she was.

She tried to catch his eye, but the crowd was too thick.

"Have you *seen* her?" the masked guy asked a couple right in front of Blaise. "I want to *knooooow. . . .*"

The couple split like bowling pins. Blaise stood exposed, tall and elegant in her black suit, lights shimmering off her midnight hair.

"Here I am, Randy," she said. "What is it you want to know?"

Randy Marik stopped, panting. His breath made a muffled noise against the plastic. The rest of the huge room was eerily silent.

Thea moved closer, walking silently. Eric was pulling in from the other side, and he saw her for the first time. He shook his head at her and mouthed, "Stay away."

Yeah. And you're going to tackle him armed with three party cups of punch. She gave him a look and mouthed, *"You* stay away."

Randy's hand was trembling, making the razor flash. His chest was heaving.

"What *is* it, Randy?" Blaise said. The toe of one high heeled shoe tapped the floor impatiently.

"I feel bad," Randy said. It was almost a moan. Suddenly his head didn't seem well connected to his neck. "I miss you."

His voice made Thea's flesh creep. He sounded like a person with the body of an eighteen-year-old and the mind of a four-year-old.

"I cry all the time," he said.

With his left hand, he pulled off the Halloween mask. Kevin recoiled. Thea herself felt a wave of horror.

He was crying *blood*. Bloody streams ran down from each of his eyes, mingling with regular tears.

A spell? Thea wondered. Then she thought, no; he's cut himself.

That was it. He'd made two crescent-shaped incisions under his eyes and the blood was coming from them.

The rest of his face was ghastly, too. He was white as a corpse and there was fuzzy stubble on his chin. His eyes stared wildly. And his hair, which had always been strawberry blond and silky, stood up all over his head like bleached hay.

"You came all the way from New Hampshire to tell me *that?*" Blaise said. She rolled her eyes.

Randy let out a sobbing breath.

This seemed to make Kevin braver. "Look, man, I don't know who you are—but you'd better keep away from her," he said. "Why don't you go home and sober up?"

It was a mistake. The wild eyes above the blood-stained cheeks focused on him.

"Who are *you?*" Randy said thickly, advancing a step. "Who . . . are . . . *you?*"

"Kevin, move!" Thea said urgently.

It was too late. The hand with the razor flashed out, lightning quick. Blood spurted from Kevin's face.

CHAPTER
6

Kevin howled, clapping a hand to his cheek. "He cut me! This guy cut me!" Blood ran between his fingers.

Randy lifted the razor again.

Thea reached out with her mind. Not reached. She *leaped*. It was completely instinctive; she was scared to death, and all she could think of was that he was going to kill Kevin, and maybe Blaise, too.

She caught—something. Pain and grief and fury that seemed to be bouncing around like a baboon in a cage. She could hold it for only an instant, but in that instant Eric threw two cups of punch in Randy's face. Randy yelled and turned away from Kevin, toward Eric.

Thea felt a surge of pure terror. Randy slashed with the razor, but Eric was fast; he jumped back out of the way, circling to get behind Randy. Randy wheeled and slashed again. They were doing a macabre dance, going round and round.

Thea felt as if the fear was winding tighter inside her with each turn. But Eric kept out of the way of the flashing razor until a rush of movement on the dance floor caught her eye. It was Mr. Adkins and two other teachers. They converged on Randy and there was a lot of confusion. When it was over, Randy was on the ground.

Sirens wailed outside, coming closer. Eric stepped away from the pile on the floor.

Breathing hard, he looked at Thea. She nodded that she was all right, then shut her eyes.

She felt limp and wrung out and awful. They were going to take Randy away now, and she didn't think there was much help for him. He definitely seemed too far gone.

At that moment she was ashamed of being a witch.

"All right, people," Mr. Adkins was saying. "Let's move out of here. Let's get this place cleared." He looked at Blaise, who was bending over a seated Kevin, holding a napkin to his cheek. "You two can stay." Then he put a hand on Blaise's shoulder. "Are you okay here?"

Blaise looked up with wide, tragic gray eyes. "I think so," she said bravely.

Mr. Adkins swallowed. His hand on Blaise's shoulder squeezed. Thea heard him mutter something like, "Poor kid."

Oh, give me a break, Thea thought. But a small, selfish part of her was relieved. Blaise wasn't going to get in trouble over this one; neither of them was going to get expelled. Grandma wasn't going to be disgraced in front of the Inner Circle.

And Blaise *did* seem worried about Kevin. She was bending over him again solicitously. As if she really cared.

Thea slipped past a teacher's outstretched arm. *"Are* you okay?" she whispered to Blaise.

Blaise looked up enigmatically. That was when Thea saw that she had a tiny vial concealed in the napkin. It was full of blood.

"You . . ." Thea couldn't find the words.

Blaise made a slight grimace that meant: *I know. But it was just too good a chance to miss.*

Thea backed up and ran into Eric. He put a steadying arm around her.

"Is she all right?"

"She's fine. *I* have to get out of here."

Eric looked into her face. He was rumpled: his hair mussed, his eyes dark. All he said was, "Let's go."

They passed Vivienne and Selene on the way out. Thea had to give them credit; they both looked shocked and unhappy. The question was, would it last?

Dani was in the parking lot with John Finkelstein. "I'm going home," she said significantly to Thea, and tossed something into a clump of bitterbrush.

It was an empty vial.

Thea felt a tiny uncoiling of relief. She touched Dani's arm lightly. "Thanks."

Dani looked back at the cafeteria. "I wonder what it was he wanted to know?" she murmured.

And just then a howl came from the lighted doorway, as if answering her question. It didn't sound like a person; it sounded like an animal in anguish.

"Whyyyyyy?"

Thea turned blindly and almost ran for Eric's jeep.

When they were driving on darkened streets, Eric said quietly, "I'm presuming he was an old boyfriend?"

"Last month's."

Eric glanced at her. "He was pretty messed up, poor guy."

And *that*, Thea thought, summed it up nicely. He was pretty messed up forever. Poor guy.

"It's Blaise," she said. She hadn't meant to talk to him about this, but the words were so crowded in her throat that she thought she'd burst if she didn't let them out. "She does this and *does* this, and I can't stop her. She picks guys up everywhere, and they fall in love with her, and then she dumps them."

"Love? Hm," Eric said.

Thea looked at him, astonished. He was looking straight ahead, his long, supple fingers steady on the wheel.

Well. And I thought you were so naive. Maybe you see more than I realized.

"It's a kind of love," she said. "It's like—do you know, in ancient Greece they worshiped the goddess Aphrodite. She was the goddess of love—and the thing about her was that she was absolutely merciless." Thea shook her head. "I saw this play once about a queen named Phaedra. And Aphrodite made her fall in love with her own stepson, and by the end of the play just about everybody was dead on the stage. But Aphrodite just kept smiling. Because she was just doing what a goddess does—the same way that a tornado rips houses apart or a fire burns down a forest."

She stopped. Her chest was aching and she didn't have any breath left. But in a way she felt better, as if some pressure had been relieved.

"And you think Blaise is like that."

"Yes. Sort of a natural force that can't help itself. Does that sound completely crazy?"

"Actually, no." Eric gave a wry smile. "Nature's rough. Hawks grab rabbits. Male lions kill cubs. It's a jungle out there."

"But that doesn't make it right. Maybe for goddesses and animals, but not when it gets to the level of humans." It was a moment before she realized what she'd said. She was using "humans" to mean "people."

"Well, humans aren't very far from animals, after all," Eric said softly.

Thea sagged back against the seat. She was still confused and unhappy, but what scared her most was that she felt a strong urge to keep talking to Eric about it. He seemed to *understand* so well . . . better than anybody else ever had. And not only to understand, but to care.

"I know what you need," Eric said suddenly, brightening. "I was going to suggest we go to the late buffet at Harrah's, but I know something better."

Thea glanced at the clock, saw that it was almost eleven. "What?"

"Puppy therapy."

"What?"

He just grinned and turned the jeep south. They pulled up at a modest gray building with a sign that read SUN CITY ANIMAL HOSPITAL.

"This is where you work."

"Yup. We can let Pilar off early," Eric said, getting out and unlocking the front door of the building. "Come on."

A pretty girl with shoulder-length brown hair looked up from behind the office counter. Thea recognized her as Pilar Osorio from school. A quiet girl who looked like a good student.

"How was the dance?" she said. Thea thought her eyes lingered on Eric wistfully as she said it.

Eric shrugged. "Pretty awful, to tell the truth. There was a fight and we left." Thea noticed he didn't mention his part in stopping the fight.

"How awful," Pilar said sympathetically—but Thea thought she wasn't entirely sorry that the dance hadn't gone well.

"Yeah. So how's our boy?"

"Okay—a little hyper. You might want to take him for a walk later." Pilar picked up her jacket. She nodded politely to Thea as she headed for the door. "See you Monday."

She likes him.

When the door was shut, Thea looked around the office. "So the clinic's not open."

"No, but somebody has to stay overnight when we've got animals boarding here." He gave her the grin again. "Follow me."

He led her through an exam room into a corridor

and then to a kennel room at the back. Thea looked around with interest. She'd never been in the inner sanctum of an animal hospital before.

There were several dog runs. Eager whining was coming from the last.

Eric looked at her mischievously. "Three, two, one . . ."

He opened the cage. A big Labrador puppy tumbled out, tail wagging frantically. He was a beautiful color that ranged from deep gold on his back to almost white on his legs and paws.

"Hey, Bud," Eric said. "Hey, pal; who's a good boy?" He looked at Thea solemnly. "This is the ultimate cuddle dog."

Thea collapsed on the sheet vinyl floor and made a lap, holding both arms out.

"Uh—your dress—" Eric began mildly, but the puppy was already in midair. Thea caught him and he crawled up her, legs on her shoulders, hot breath blowing in her ear.

"I think I'm in love," Thea gasped, her arms full of warm, heavy puppy sweetness.

Happiness surrounded her. She didn't have to try to merge with the puppy's mind; he practically took over by force. All his thoughts were good ones, and they were all about *now*. About how terrific everything smelled this minute, and how great that scratch behind the ear felt on a fleabite.

Good feelings, happy feelings . . . I really like this big bald dog . . . Wonder which of us is dominant?

The puppy bit her and Thea play-bit him back.

"Wrong; I'm the pack leader," she informed him, holding his jowls.

There was only one odd thing. She could see the way the world looked to the pup—and there was nothing on the right. Just a void.

"Is there something wrong with his eyes?"

"You noticed the cataract. Lots of people don't see that right away. Yeah, he's blind in the right eye. When he gets older he may come back for surgery." Eric sat back against the wall, grinning madly. "You've really got a way with animals," he said. "But you don't own any pets?"

The question was gentle, not intrusive. Thea said absently, "Well, usually just temporary ones. I pick them up and when they're cured I put them back— or find homes for them if they *want* to be pets."

"You cure them."

Once again, the question was gentle, but Thea felt a little shock. Why couldn't she guard her tongue around this guy? She looked up and found he was looking at her steadily and searchingly, his green eyes alert.

She took a breath. "I feed them, take them to the vet if they need it. Then I wait until they heal up."

He nodded, but the searching look didn't go away. "Did you ever think of being a vet yourself?"

Thea had to look down. She bluffed by kissing the puppy.

"Uh, not really," she muttered into blond fur.

"But you've got a *gift*. Look, I've got some material on U.C. Davis. They have a great undergraduate program—and their graduate school is one of the best in the country. It's not easy to get in, but you could do it. I know you could."

"I wouldn't bet on it," Thea muttered. She had several dramatic blotches on her academic record— like four expulsions.

But that wasn't the real problem. The real problem was that witches weren't veterinarians. They just *weren't*.

She could choose to specialize in gems or herbs or ritual clothing; in chants or runes or research or amulets . . . in hundreds of things, but nothing taught at U.C. Davis.

"It's hard to explain," Thea said. She didn't have much room left to be surprised, or she'd have been surprised to find she *wanted* to explain to a human. "It's just—my family wouldn't really approve. They want me to be something else."

Eric opened his mouth, then shut it again.

The puppy sneezed.

"Well—maybe you could help me with *my* application sometime," Eric said at last. "I'm trying to do the essay question and dying."

You sneak, Thea thought.

"Maybe," she said.

At that moment a buzzer sounded—far away but insistent. Bud barked.

"What the . . . that's the outside buzzer," Eric said. "But nobody should be here at this time of night." He got up and headed for the front of the building. Thea followed, her fingertips just brushing Bud's head to control him.

Eric opened the door, then stepped back in surprise.

"Rosamund . . . what are you *doing* here? Does Mom know you're out?"

Something like a miniature whirlwind entered the waiting room. It was a kid, a little girl with a mop of sandy hair sticking out from under a baseball cap. She was carrying a rolled-up blue blanket, and what could be seen of her expression under the hair was ferocious.

"Mom said Madame Curie wasn't really sick, but she is. Call Dr. Joan." With that, the kid marched into the office and dumped the blue blanket on the counter, pushing aside a clipboard and some vaccination reminder cards.

"Hey. Don't." When she ignored him, Eric looked at Thea. "Uh, this is my sister Rosamund. And I don't know how she got here—"

"I rode my bike and I want Madame Curie fixed *now.*"

Bud was rearing up and trying to sniff the blue blanket. Thea pushed him down gently. "Who's Madame Curie?"

"Madame Curie is a guinea pig," Eric said. He touched the blanket. "Roz—Dr. Joan is gone. She's out of town at a conference."

Rosamund's ferocious expression never wavered, but her chin began to quiver.

"Okay, listen. I'll take a look at Madame Curie now, see if I can see anything. But first we have to call Mom and let her know you're alive." He reached for the phone.

"I'll take Bud back," Thea said. "I think he thinks Madame Curie is lunch." She led the puppy into the back room and coaxed him into the run with a promise of extra petting later.

When she came back to the office, Eric was bent over a small brown-and-white guinea pig. He looked frustrated.

"Well, there's *something* wrong with her—I guess. She seems weaker than usual and sort of lethargic. . . ." Suddenly he jerked his hand back with a yelp.

"Not *too* lethargic," he said, eyeing the blood welling up from his thumb. He wiped it on a tissue and bent over the guinea pig again.

"She's in a bad mood," Rosamund said. "And she's not eating right. I told you yesterday she was sick."

"No, you didn't," Eric said calmly. "You told me she was tired of living under patriarchy."

"Well, she *is* tired. *And* she's sick. *Do* something."

"Kid, I don't know what to do yet. Hang on." He bent closer to the little animal, muttering to himself. "She's not coughing . . . so it's not strep. Her lymph nodes are okay . . . but her joints seem swollen. Now, that's weird."

Rosamund was watching him, her green eyes full of fierce trust. Eyes like Eric's, Thea realized.

She reached out gently and just touched the guinea pig's soft fur with her fingers. Her mind reached gently, too.

Frightened-little-animal thoughts. The guinea pig didn't like being here, wanted the sawdust of her cage, wanted safety. She didn't like the clinical smells, didn't like huge, strange fingers descending from the sky.

Home-place, nest-place, she was thinking. And then, something odd. A concept—more smell and taste than picture. Madame Curie was imagining eating something . . . something crunchy and slightly sharp. Eating and eating and eating.

"Is there some treat she really likes?" Thea asked doubtfully. "Something like cabbage?"

Eric blinked, then straightened up as if he'd gotten an electric shock. His green eyes stared straight into hers. "That's it! You're brilliant!"

"What's it?"

"What you said. She's got *scurvy!*" He dashed out of the office and came back with a thick book full of small print. "Yeah—here it is. Anorexia, lethargy, enlarged limb joints . . . she's got all the symptoms." He turned pages feverishly and then said triumphantly, "All we have to do is give her some of those veggies, or maybe some ascorbic acid in her water."

Scurvy—wasn't that a disease sailors used to get? When they were on long trips with no fresh fruits or vegetables? And ascorbic acid was . . . "Vitamin C!"

"Yeah! It's been hot and we've got hard water at our house—all that could deplete the vitamin C in her diet. But it's easy to fix." Then Eric looked at Thea and shook his head wonderingly. "I've been studying for years, besides working here, and you just *look* at the animal and you know. How do you *do* that?"

"She asked Madame Curie," Rosamund said flatly.

Thea gave her a wary glance. How come this whole

family was so observant? "Ha ha," she said, her voice light.

"I like you," Rosamund said, just as flatly as before. "Now where can I get some cabbage?"

"Go look in the vaccine fridge in back," Eric said. "If there isn't any, we can always use vitamin drops."

Rosamund trotted off. Eric watched her, openly fond.

"She's an interesting kid," Thea said.

"She's sort of a genius. Also the world's smallest militant feminist. She's suing the local Boy Trekkers, you know. They won't let her in, and the Girl Trekkers don't trek. They do macramé."

Thea looked at him. "And what do you think of that?"

"Me? I drive her to the lawyer's office whenever Mom can't make it. I figure it stops her griping. Besides, she's right."

Simple as that, Thea thought. She watched Eric as he folded the blue blanket, and heard a voice in her mind like the voice of an announcer describing a game-show prize.

Now. Look at this guy. He's tender but intense. Brave. Profoundly insightful. Shy but with a wicked sense of humor. He's smart, he's honest, he's an animal lover. . . .

He's human.

I don't care.

She was feeling—well, strange. As if she'd been breathing too much yemonja root. The air seemed sweet and heavy and *tingly* somehow, as if laced with tropical electricity.

"Eric . . ."

And she found herself touching the back of his hand.

He let go of the blanket instantly and turned his hand to close on hers. He wasn't looking at her, though. He was still staring at the office desk. His chest heaved.

"Eric?"

"Sometimes I think if I blink, you'll disappear."

Oh, Eileithyia, Thea thought. Oh, Aphrodite. I'm in terrible trouble.

The thing was, it was terrible and wonderful. She felt awkward and tremendously safe at once, scared to death and not scared of anything. And what she wanted was so simple. If he only felt the same, everything would be all right.

"I just can't even imagine life without you anymore, but I'm so afraid you'll go away," Eric said, still looking fatalistically at the computer on the desk. Then he turned to her. "Are you mad?"

Thea shook her head. Her heart was threatening to leave her body. When she met his eyes it was as if some circuit had closed. They were connected, now, and being pulled together as if Aphrodite herself was gathering them into her arms.

And then everything was warm and wonderful. Better than holding the puppy, because Eric could hold her, too. And the thrills of fear that had been shooting through her seemed somehow to burst like fireworks and turn into exhilaration.

Her cheek was against Eric's. And she'd never felt anything so blissful before. Eric's cheek was smooth and firm—and she was safe here, loved here. She could rest like this forever. Peace filled her like cool water. They were two birds enfolding each other with their wings.

Swans mate for life . . . and when they see their mate, they *know*, she thought. That's what happened in the desert. We knew each other; it was as if we each could see the other one's soul. Once you see into someone's soul, you're attached forever.

Yeah, and there's a word for it in the Night World, part of her mind said, trying to shatter her peace. The soulmate principle. You're trying to say that your one and only is a human?

But Thea couldn't be frightened, not now. She felt insulated from the Night World and the human world both. She and Eric formed their own reality; and it was enough just to stand here and *breathe* and to feel his breathing, without worrying about the future. . . .

A door creaked and a blast of cool air blew in.

Thea's eyes were startled open. And then her heart gave a terrible lurch and started thudding painfully.

It wasn't the door that Rosamund had gone through. It was the front door, which Eric must have left unlocked. And Blaise was standing there in the waiting room.

CHAPTER
7

I've been looking *everywhere* for you," Blaise said. "I had to call Mrs. Ross to find out you were here."

Her black hair was wild and windblown, tumbling over her shoulders. She had taken off her red bow tie and unbuttoned the top button of her dress shirt. There was color in her cheeks and dark light in her gray eyes. She looked extremely beautiful and very, very witchy.

Thea and Eric had moved apart and Thea had the feeling they were both blushing.

"We were just . . ." Eric said. "Um. Heh." While Blaise scrutinized him, he picked up the blue blanket and started refolding it. "Uh, can I show you around?"

"I don't care much for animals unless they've been shish-kebabed." Blaise surveyed the room with one hand on her hip.

Oh, she's in a *terrific* mood.

Thea's palms were getting damp. She wasn't sure what Blaise thought of the embrace she'd walked in on . . . but Thea was *supposed* to be leading Eric on, wasn't she?

Her eye fell on the Kleenex daubed with Eric's blood. Unobtrusively, she reached for it and crumpled it in her hand.

"So you left the dance," she said to Blaise. "Where's . . ." Who'd actually been Blaise's date tonight? Sergio? Kevin? Someone else?

"There is no dance," Blaise said. "They shut it down. Leave it to Randy—he was always a royal pain." Then her face changed; she blinked and put on a sweet smile. "And who are you, darling?"

In the doorway to the corridor, Rosamund backed up, Madame Curie clutched to her chest. She didn't say a word, but her hostile green eyes never left Blaise.

"Uh, sorry," Eric said. "That's my sister. She's— shy."

"So this is a family affair," Blaise said. "How nice."

Thea said, "I think it's time to be going home." She needed to talk to Eric, but alone, not with a disgruntled munchkin and a suspicious witch looking on.

She glanced at Eric, feeling a little shy herself. He looked the same.

"Well—see you at school."

"Yeah." Suddenly he smiled. "You know, that's something else I was going to mention. If you're even thinking about going to Davis, you might want to get into honors zoology. It's a good class."

"Um—we'll see." She was aware of Blaise watching her.

But outside, all Blaise said was, "Sorry if I was rude. But I've been looking all over for you, so I could tell you what a great time I wasn't having. And"—she shook her midnight hair out with a charming smile—"it's so much *fun* to be a bitch when you want to be."

Thea sighed, then stopped in her tracks. "Blaise, the car!"

Kevin's silver-gray Porsche looked as if it had been through a war. The front bumper was caved in, the passenger door was mangled, and the windshield was cracked.

"I had a little trouble," Blaise said coolly. "It's all right, though; I met a guy tonight named Luke Price, who's got a Maserati." She looked at Thea, then added, "You don't *disapprove*, do you? Of treating humans that way?"

"No—of course not. I just don't want to get expelled again."

"It's not illegal to have an accident. Here, you have to get in through the driver's side now."

She drove, not seeming to choose any particular direction. Thea sat quietly, acutely aware of the probing glances cast her way every so often.

"So," Blaise said at last in her silkiest voice, "did you get *it?*"

"What?"

"Don't be funny."

Thea held out her hand with the crumpled Kleenex on her palm. "I didn't fill the vial; that was ridiculous. But I used my ingenuity and got enough."

"Hmm." Blaise's tapering fingers, tipped with blood-red nails, closed delicately on the tissue. Startled, Thea snatched it back and the Kleenex tore. She ended up with only a corner.

"Hey—"

"What's the problem? I just want it for safekeeping," Blaise said smoothly. "And so how did everything else go?"

"Fine," Thea said. Her palms were getting damp, but she managed to keep her voice airy. "I think he's hooked," she added, trying to imitate Blaise's most languid and arrogant tones.

"Oh, really?" They had ended up on the strip, which meant the car was now crawling through traffic. Neon highlighted the curious half-smile on Blaise's lips. "And what was that about Davis?"

"Nothing. It's where he's going to college, so of course he'd like me to be with him."

"He's already thinking about the future. Well, that was fast work. Congratulations."

Thea didn't like the way she said it. More than ever, she wanted to protect Eric from Blaise—but she wasn't sure how. It depended on how much Blaise suspected.

"You know, I think it's the pop that's the most fun," Blaise went on reminiscently. "Human boys are all different—but in the end, they're all the same. And when they give in completely, you can almost hear it. There's a 'pop.' Like a balloon breaking."

Thea swallowed, staring at the huge golden lion in front of the MGM Grand Hotel. Its green eyes reminded her of Eric. "Really? Sounds interesting."

"Oh, it is. And after the pop, they just kind of collapse, and everything they are, their whole *self*, just sort of pours out in this internal hemorrhage. And after that, of course, they're useless. Like a stag that's too old to mate. They're just—over."

"How nice."

"You know, I think Eric's ready for that pop. He's already in love with you; I could see that. I think it's time."

Thea just sat. A vampire girl, wearing a dress with a black rose design, threaded her way through stopped traffic. Finally, Thea said, "Blaise . . ."

"What, is that a problem with you? Are you having difficulty with that? Are you a little soft on him, maybe? Are you a little *too* fond of him?"

"Blaise—"

"Are you in love with him?"

Shock waves went through Thea, and the last question seemed to vibrate in the air.

At last she whispered, "Don't be ridiculous."

"And don't *you* try to fool me. Remember who you're talking to. I know that dopey look you get when you're mooning over some animal. I saw the way you were holding him."

Thea felt desperate. It wasn't just Blaise she was afraid of here. Night World law couldn't be clearer about the penalty for loving a human.

Death. Not only for her, but for Eric, too.

There was only one thing Thea could do. She turned and looked at her cousin directly.

"All right, Blaise, you do know me. We've always been like sisters, and I know that however you act sometimes, you still love me—"

"Of course I do," Blaise said impatiently, and Thea realized that was part of the problem. In the changing light of the Bally hotel's neon pillars, she could see that Blaise's eyes were wet. She was *frightened* for Thea—and angry at being frightened.

Thea grabbed her cousin's hand. "Then you have to listen to me." It was a naked plea. "Blaise—when I first met Eric, something *happened*. I can't explain it—I can't even really describe it. But there was a connection. And I know this is going to sound insane, and I know you're not going to like it, but . . ." She had to stop to breathe. "Blaise, what if you found your soulmate, and they were something that everybody said you shouldn't love. . . ."

She stopped again, this time because Blaise had frozen. For a moment they both just sat, and then, very slowly, Blaise withdrew her hand from Thea's.

"Found . . . your . . . soulmate?" she said.

Warmth pooled in Thea's eyes. She had never felt so alone. "I think so," she whispered.

Blaise turned to face the windshield. Purple light shone on her black hair. "This is more serious than I thought."

The tears overflowed. "But will you help me?"

Blaise tapped her slender fingers on the steering wheel a few times. Finally she said, "Of course I'll help you. I *have* to. We're like sisters—I would never abandon you when you're in trouble."

Thea was so relieved she felt dizzy. Paradoxically, it made her cry more. "I've just been so scared. . . . Ever since it happened, I've been trying to figure things out." She hiccupped. Blaise was looking at her again, smiling, gray eyes glittering oddly. "Blaise?"

"I'm going to help you," Blaise said, still smiling, "by getting him myself. And then I'm going to kill him for putting my sister in danger."

There was a moment when everything inside Thea seemed absolutely still—and the next instant it all exploded into chaos.

"Never," she said. "Do you hear me, *sister? Never."*

Blaise stayed calm, driving. "I know you don't think it's best—now. But one day you'll thank me."

"Blaise, *listen to me.* If you do anything to him—if you hurt him—it's me you're hurting."

"You'll get over it." In the rainbow light of the Riviera, Blaise looked like some ancient goddess of fate. "It's better to hurt a little now than to be executed later."

Thea was so angry she was shaking. So angry that she made a mistake. If she'd kept on arguing the same points, she thought later, Blaise might eventually have started to listen. But she was furious and terrified and she blurted out, "Well, I don't think you *can* do it. I don't think you could take him from me if you tried."

Blaise stared, as if caught for once at a loss for words. Then she threw back her head and laughed.

"Thea," she said. "I can take *any* boy from *anybody.*

Any time, any place, any way I want to. That's what I *do*."

"Not this time. Eric loves me, and you can't change that. You can't take him."

Blaise was wearing a secret smile. But she said only two words as she turned off the strip and onto darkened streets again.

"Watch me."

Thea didn't sleep well. She kept seeing Randy Marik's face, and when she dreamed, it turned into Eric's face, blood-streaked and vacant-eyed.

She woke up to see sunshine streaming in the room.

It was a bedroom with a split personality. One side was fairly neat and decorated in pale blues and spring greens. The other side was messy and was decorated in *the* color, the primal color, the one that roused emotions, that meant passion and hatred both. Red.

And usually Blaise was lying on that side underneath her red velvet Ralph Lauren bedspread, but this morning she was gone already. A bad omen. Blaise only got up early for a reason.

Thea got dressed and went downstairs warily.

The shop was empty except for Tobias sitting gloomily in his usual place beside the cash register. He grunted when Thea said hello and went on staring at the wall, one hand clutching his curly brown hair. Wishing, undoubtedly, to be outside on the weekend like other nineteen-year-old guys.

Thea went into the workshop.

Blaise was sitting at the long table, wearing earphones and humming to herself. A project was spread in front of her.

Thea stalked up close.

She could see right away that it was beautiful. Blaise was a genius at creating jewelry, most of it based on ancient designs. She made necklaces of bees and butterflies, spiraling flowers, serpents, leaping dolphins. It was all alive, all joyous . . . all magical.

That was where the real genius came in. Blaise put each element of the piece together with a purpose in mind. The gems were chosen to enhance each other: ruby for desire, black opal for obsession, topaz for yearning, garnet for heat. And asteria, the smoke-gray form of sapphire with a six-pointed star. Blaise's stone, just the color of her eyes.

Blaise had them all laid out loose. But her magic wasn't just in the gems. Interwoven into every piece were herb caches, tiny compartments that could be filled with potions or powders. She could literally *drench* the jewelry in sorcery.

Even the design itself could be a spell. Every line, every curve, every flower stem could have a meaning, could make the eye follow a pattern that was as powerful as any symbol traced on the floor in chalk. Just looking at the piece could be enough to charm you.

Right now Blaise was working on a necklace to knock you dead.

Thea could see it taking shape. Blaise used the lost wax method of jewelry-making, which meant that she carved out her pieces in stiff blue wax before casting them in silver or copper or gold. What she was carving now was breathtaking. Heart-stopping. An intricate masterpiece that was going to have roughly the same effect as Aphrodite's magic girdle— which meant no male was going to be able to look at it without falling under the spell.

And she had some of Eric's blood. The vital ingredient that meant she'd be able to personalize this spell for him.

The one good thing was that it would take Blaise a few days to finish this piece. But once it was done. . . .

Eric didn't have a chance in Hades.

Thea backed up, not knowing—and not caring— whether Blaise had noticed her. She headed blindly for her bedroom.

She and Eric were soulmates. But Blaise was, in some ways, Aphrodite herself. And who could resist that?

What am I going to do?

She had a little of Eric's blood herself on the corner of the tissue. But she could never outmatch Blaise in creating love spells. Blaise had years of experience and a natural talent that left everyone else in the dust.

So I have to think of something else. Something to keep her from getting to him in the first place. To protect him . . .

Thea straightened up.

I can't. It's too dangerous. The summoning spells aren't for maidens. Even the Inner Circle has to be careful with those.

But Grandma has the materials. I know she does. I've seen the box.

It may kill me even to try.

An odd serenity came over her. If she concentrated on that—on the risk—she felt better than if she thought about what Gran would say if she found out. She wasn't afraid to face danger for Eric. And as long as she kept thinking about *that*, she could block out the thought that her idea was not only dangerous, but *wrong*.

This time she went down the stairs almost as if she were sleepwalking. Calm and detached.

"Toby, where's Gran?"

He lifted his head a bare inch. "She went to see Thierry Descouedres, something about his land. Told me to come and pick her up tonight."

Thierry was a vampire and a Night Lord. He owned a lot of the land northeast of Las Vegas—but what did Gran have to do with that?

It didn't matter. The important thing was that Gran wouldn't be back all day.

"Well, then, why don't you go out and have some fun? I can watch the shop."

Tobias looked at her with dazed blue eyes—and then his round face lit up. "Seriously? You'd do that? I could kiss you. Let's see, I'll go visit Kishi . . . no, maybe Zoe . . . no, maybe Sheena. . . ."

Like all boy witches, he was in tremendous demand with the girl witches in town.

Still muttering, he checked his wallet, grabbed the car keys, and headed for the door as if Thea might change her mind any second. "I'll be back in time to pick her up, I promise," he said hastily and was out the door.

The instant he was gone, Thea turned the sign on the door to CLOSED, locked up, and tiptoed to the counter.

It was in the locked lower shelf, an iron chest that looked five hundred years old. Thea picked it up with an effort—it was *heavy*. With her teeth gritted and her eyes on the bead curtain that separated the store from Grandma's workshop, she staggered up the stairs.

She made two other trips downstairs to gather materials. The bead curtain never stirred.

Last, she went to Gran's bedroom. On a nail near the headboard was a heavy ring with dozens of keys. Thea took it. Back in her own bedroom she shut the door and stuffed a towel underneath so Blaise wouldn't smell the smoke.

Okay, now let's get this thing open.

She sat crosslegged on the floor in front of the chest. It wasn't hard to find the key that would fit the lock—she just looked for the oldest and crudest iron key on the ring. It fit perfectly and the chest opened.

Inside was a bronze box, and inside *that* a silver box.

And inside the silver box was an ancient book with yellowing, brittle pages, and a small green bottle with wax and ribbons securing its cork. There were also thirty or forty amulets. Thea picked one up and examined it.

A lock of blond hair had been twisted and woven

into a knot, and then sealed in that shape with a round piece of clay. The clay was dark earthy red, and Thea touched it reverently. It had been made with mud—and the blood of a witch. An entire Circle had probably worked on this for weeks: charging the blood, chanting, mixing it with secret ingredients, baking it in a ritual fire.

I'm touching a witch, Thea thought. The very essence of somebody who's been dead hundreds of years.

The cabalistic sign stamped on the front of the amulet was supposed to show *who* the witch was. But lots of the pieces of clay were so worn that Thea couldn't make out any trace of a symbol.

Don't worry. Find a description of somebody in the book, and then match the amulet to them.

She turned the fragile pages of the book carefully, trying to read the spidery, faded writing.

Ix U Sihnal, Annie Butter, Markus Klingelsmith . . . no, they all sound too dangerous. *Lucio Cagliostro*— maybe. But I don't really want an alchemist. *Dewi Ratih, Omiya Inoshishi* . . . wait a minute. *Phoebe Garner.*

She scanned the page on Phoebe eagerly. A gentle girl from England who had lived before the Burning Times and had kept familiars. She'd died young of tuberculosis, but had been considered a blessing by everyone who'd known her—even humans, who appreciated her ability to deflect spells from her village. Human villagers had mourned at her grave.

Perfect, Thea thought.

Then, she began scrabbling through the amulets,

looking for one with the same symbol impressed on the clay as the book showed by Phoebe's name.

There it was! She cradled the amulet in her palm. Phoebe's hair had been auburn and very fine.

Okay. Now get the balefire ready.

It had to be made from oak and ash, the two kinds of wood that had been burned to bake the clay. Thea put the dry sticks in her grandmother's largest bronze bowl and lit them.

Now add quassia chips, blessed thistle, mandrake root. Those were just for general power raising. The real magic was in the tiny bottle that had been carved out of a single piece of malachite. It was the summoning potion, and Thea had no idea at all what was in it.

She dug at the wax with her fingernails until the cork twisted freely. Then she paused, her hands shaking with every beat of her pulse.

Up until now, she'd only examined things she shouldn't: bad but forgivable. *Now* she was going to kindle a forbidden fire . . . and that *wasn't* forgivable. If the elders discovered what she'd done . . .

She pulled the cork out.

CHAPTER

8

A sharp, acrid odor assaulted her nostrils. She had to blink away tears as she held the bottle over the fire and very carefully tipped it.

One drop, two drops, *three*.

The fire flared, burning blue.

It was ready. The balefire that was the only way to get a spirit from the other side—apart from crossing the veil and fetching it back yourself.

Thea took Phoebe's amulet in both hands and snapped it, cracking the clay and breaking the seal. Then, holding the broken amulet over the fire, she said the words of power she'd heard the elders speaking last Samhain.

"May I be given the Power of the Words of Hecate."

Instantly, she found words coming to her, rolling off her tongue. She heard them as if it were somebody else talking.

From beyond the veil . . . I call you back!
Through the mist of years . . . I call you back!
From the airy void . . . I call you back!
Through the narrow path . . . I call you back!
To the heart of the flame . . . I call you back!
Come speedily, conveniently, and without delay!

She felt a rumbling vibration like an earthquake
rock the floor. Above the ordinary fire different
flames seemed to burn; cold, ghostly flames that were
pale blue and violet and rose to lick at her knuckles.

She started to open her hands, to let the amulet
fall into the magical flame. But just as she was about
to do it, there was a bang.

The door to her bedroom swung open, and for the
second time in twelve hours she found herself horrified to see Blaise.

"The whole place is shaking—what are you *doing?*"

"Blaise—just stay back!"

Blaise stared. Her jaw dropped and she lunged forward. *"What are you doing?"*

"It's almost finished—"

"You're crazy!" Blaise grabbed at the amulet in
Thea's hands, and then, when Thea snatched her
hands back, at the silver box.

"Leave it alone!" Thea grabbed the other side of
the box. They were struggling with it, each trying to
pull it from the other. Fire scorched Thea's hands.

"Let *go!*" Blaise shouted, trying to twist the box
away. "I'm warning you—"

Thea's fingers were damp with sweat. The box
slipped.

That was when it happened.

The silver box flipped in Blaise's hands, sending a spray of amulets everywhere. Locks of gray hair, black hair, red hair, all flying. Most of them hit the floor—but one landed directly in the balefire.

Thea heard a crack as the clay seal broke.

For one second she was frozen, then she plunged her hand into the fire. But the clay was already burning—not red hot, but white hot. She couldn't close her fingers around it. For just an instant she seemed to see a symbol etched in blue flames, and then a flash like sheet lightning exploded from the fire. It knocked her into Blaise's bed and Blaise into the wall.

The lightning formed a column and *something* shot out.

Thea didn't so much see it as sense it. A wraith shape that tore around the room like a blast of arctic wind. It sent books and articles of clothing flying. When it reached the window, it seemed to pause for an instant, as if gathering itself, and then it shot through as if the glass didn't exist.

It was gone.

"Great Mother of Life," Blaise whispered from against the wall. She was staring at the window with huge luminous eyes—and she was scared. Blaise was scared.

That was when Thea realized how bad things were.

"What have we done?" she whispered.

"What have *we* done—what have *you* done, that's the question," Blaise snapped, sitting up and looking more like her ordinary self. "What *was* that thing?"

Defensively, Thea gestured at the scattered amulets. "What do you think? A witch."

"But *who?*"

"How should I know?" Thea almost yelled, fear giving way to anger. "*This* is the one I was going to call back." She snatched up the auburn hair and cracked amulet of Phoebe Garner. "*That* one was just whichever one fell out when you grabbed the box."

"Don't try to make this my fault. *You're* the one doing forbidden spells. *You're* the one summoning ancestors. And whatever happens with that one"— Blaise pointed at the window—"*you're* the one responsible."

She got up and shook out her hair, standing tall. "And *that's* what you get for trying to sic the spirits on me!" She turned and stalked out the door.

"I wasn't trying to sic the spirits on you!" Thea shouted—but the door had already slammed shut.

Thea's anger collapsed. Feeling numb, she looked at the overturned silver box, where she had temporarily stored the tissue with Eric's blood.

I was just trying to find a protector for him. *Somebody who'd help him fend off your spells, who'd understand that he's a person even though he's a human.*

She looked forlornly around the room. Then, feeling older than Gran, she struggled to her feet and started mechanically cleaning up the mess.

When she dumped the ashes out of the bowl she found some sort of residue sticking to the bottom. She couldn't wash it off and she couldn't pry it off with a steak knife. She stashed the entire bowl under her bed.

All the while she cleaned, her mind kept churning.

Who got out? No way to know. Process of elimination wouldn't help, not with all those unmarked amulets.

What to do now? She didn't know that either.

If I tell anyone—even Gran—they'll want to know why I was trying to summon the dead. But if they find out the truth, it means death for me and Eric.

Around sunset, a limousine pulled up in the back alley. Thea saw it from her window and rushed downstairs in alarm.

Grandma was being helped out of the car by two politely expressionless vampires. Servants of Thierry's.

"Gran, what happened?"

"Nothing happened. I had a little weak spell, that's all!" She whacked at one of the vampires with her cane. "I can help myself, son!"

"Ma'am," said the vampire—who might have been three or four times Grandma's age. To Thea, he said, "Your grandmother fainted—she was pretty sick there for a while."

"And that good-for-nothing apprentice of mine never showed up," Gran said, making her way to the back door.

Thea nodded good-bye to the vampires. "Gran—it was my fault about Tobias. I let him have the day off." Her stomach, which had been clenched like a fist all day, seemed to draw even tighter now. "Are you really sick?"

"I'm good for a few years yet." She began labori-
ously working her way up the stairs. "Vampires just
don't understand old age."

"What did you go there for?"

Gran stopped to cough. "None of your business,
but I had to settle some arrangements with Thierry.
He's agreed to let the Inner Circle use his land on
Samhain."

Upstairs, Thea made some herb tea in the tiny
kitchenette. And then, when Gran was in bed with
the tea, she gathered her courage.

"Gran, when the elders call up the spirits on Samhain—how do they send them *back*?"

"Why should you want to know?" Gran said
crossly. But when Thea just looked at her, she went
on. "There are certain spells that are used for summoning—and don't you ask me what they are—and
you say those backwards to send them back. The
witch who calls a spirit has to be the one to dismiss
it."

So only I can do it. "And that's all?" Thea asked.

"Oh, of course not. It's a long process of kindling
the fire and strewing the herbs—but if you do it all
right, you can draw the spirit down from between
the standing stones and send it back where it came
from." Grandma went on muttering, but Thea had
snagged on a earlier phrase.

"From between—the standing stones . . . ?" she
got out.

"The standing stones that encircle the spirits. Well,
think, Thea! If you didn't have a circle of some kind
to hold them in, they'd just—*voom*." Gran made a

gesture. "They'd zip out and how would you ever find them again? That's why I went to Thierry today," she added, taking a noisy sip of tea. "We need a place where the sandstone forms a natural circle . . . and naturally it's up to me to arrange everything. . . ." She went on grumbling softly.

Thea felt faint.

"You *have* to be—physically close to them—to send them back?"

"Of course. You have to be within spitting distance. And don't think I don't know why you're asking."

Thea stopped breathing.

"You're planning something for Samhain—and it's probably all Blaise's idea. You two are like Maya and Hellewise. But you can forget about it right now— those spells are for the elders, not for girls." She stopped to cough. "I don't understand why you want to be crones before you're done being maidens. You ought to enjoy your youth while you have it. . . ."

Thea left her still grumbling.

She hadn't cast any kind of a circle before calling the spirit. She hadn't realized she was supposed to.

And now . . . how could she ever get close enough to the spirit to send it back?

Well—it'll just have to *stay* out in the world, she told herself bravely. Too bad . . . but it's not as if there aren't other spirits floating around out there. Maybe if it doesn't like roaming around, it'll come back.

But she was sick with guilt and disheartened. Not to mention worried—if only a little—about Gran's fainting spell.

Blaise didn't come to bed. She stayed downstairs and worked on her necklace long into the night.

On Monday, everyone at school was talking about Randy Marik and the ruined dance. The girls were annoyed about it and furious with Blaise; the boys were annoyed and furious with Randy.

"Are you okay?" Dani asked Thea after world lit class. "You look kind of pale."

Thea smiled wanly. "It was a busy weekend."

"Really? Did you do something with Eric?" The way she said "do something" alerted Thea. Dani's heart-shaped face looked as sweet and concerned as ever . . . but Thea couldn't trust even her. She was a Night Person, a witch, a human-hater.

It didn't matter. Thea was so edgy that the words just seemed to burst out. "Do something like what? Smash his car? Turn him into a toad?"

Dani looked shocked, her velvet-dark eyes wide.

Thea turned and walked quickly away.

Stupid, *stupid*, she told herself. That was so *dumb* of you. You may not have to pretend to be playing with Eric in front of Blaise anymore—but in front of the other witches you've *got* to keep acting.

She headed almost blindly for Eric's locker, ignoring the people she passed.

I've only been here a week. How can everything in my life have become so awful? I'm at war with Blaise; I've worked a forbidden spell; I don't dare talk to Gran—and I've broken Night World law.

"Thea! I was looking for you."

It was Eric's voice. Warm, eager—everything that

Thea wasn't. She turned to see green eyes flecked with dancing gray and an astonishing smile. A smile that drew her in, changing the world.

Maybe everything was going to be all right, after all.

"I called you yesterday, but I just kept getting the machine."

Thea hadn't even looked at the answering machine. "I'm sorry—there was a lot going on." Eric looked so kind that she groped for something that had been going on that she could *tell* him about. "My grandmother's been sick."

He sobered at once. "That's terrible."

"Yes." Thea fished in her backpack for the small herb pillow she'd put there this morning. Then she hesitated. "Eric . . . is there somewhere we could go to talk alone? Just for a few minutes? I want to give you something."

He blinked, then waggled his eyebrows. "Nothing I'd like better. And I know just the place. Come on."

He led her across campus to a large building that stood apart from the rest of the complex. It had a shabby look and the paint on the double doors was blistered. A banner announced in orange and black letters: DON'T MISS THE ULTIMATE HALLOWEEN PARTY.

"What is this?"

Eric, who was opening the door, put a finger to his lips. He glanced inside, then beckoned to her.

"It's the old gym. They're supposed to be renovating it as a student center, but there isn't enough money." He snorted. "Probably because they're

spending too much on renovating downtown. Now—
what was it you wanted to give me?"

"It . . ." Thea stopped dead as she took in her
surroundings. All thoughts of the herb pillow van-
ished. "Eric . . ." She stared around her, feeling a
slow wave of sickness roil through her stomach. "Is
this . . . for the Halloween party?"

"Yeah. They do a couple fund-raisers a semester
here. This is kind of a weird one—but they did it last
year and it brought in a lot."

Not weird, Thea thought numbly. Weird doesn't
begin to describe it.

Half the room was empty, just scuffed hardwood
floor, a broken basketball backboard, and exposed
pipes in the ceiling. But the other half looked like a
cross between a medieval dungeon and a casino. She
walked slowly toward it, her footsteps echoing.

Wooden booths of various sizes were decorated
with orange and black crepe paper and fake spider
webs. Thea read one banner after another.

"Fortune telling . . . Drench a Wench . . . *Bobbing
for Shrunken Heads?*"

"It's bobbing for apples really," Eric said, seeming
embarrassed. "And the gambling isn't real. You do it
all with goblin money and exchange it for prizes."

Thea couldn't stop looking at the booths. Wheel of
Torture: a money wheel with a dummy dressed like
a witch spreadeagled in the middle. Bloody Blackjack.
Devil's Darts . . . a dart game with a cork witch as
a target.

And there were witch figures everywhere. Cloth
witches on nooses hanging from the overhead pipes.

Cardboard witches leering from the tops of booths. Paper witches dancing on the wall. They were fat, skinny, white-haired, gray-haired, cross-eyed, squint-eyed, warty, funny, scary . . . and *ugly*. That was the one thing they all had in common.

That's what they think of us. Humans. All humans . . .

"Thea? Are you okay?"

Thea whirled. "No, I am not *okay*." She gestured around the room. "Will you *look* at this stuff? Do you really think it's funny? Something to party about?" Hardly aware of what she was doing, she spun him around to face The Iron Maiden—a wooden replica with rubber spikes.

"What are people going to do? Pay to step into that? Don't they realize that it used to be *real?* That *real* people were put in it, and that when the door closed, those spikes went into them, into their arms and their stomachs and their eyes . . ." She couldn't go on.

Eric looked as stricken as Dani had earlier. He'd never seen her like this. "Thea—look, I'm sorry . . . I never thought . . ."

"Or *that*." Thea gestured toward the Wheel of Torture, the words tumbling out. "Do you know how they *really* put a witch on the wheel? They broke every bone in her body so they could just thread her arms and legs through the spokes like spaghetti. Then they put the wheel on a pole and left her up there to die. . . ."

Eric's face contracted with horror. "God, Thea . . ."

"And these pictures—the witches who got tortured

didn't have green skin and evil eyes. They weren't monsters, and they didn't have anything to do with devils. They were *people*."

Eric reached out for her, but she spun away, staring at a particularly ugly hag on the wall. "Do *you* think this place is all right for a party? That this is good fun? That witches look like *that*?" She flung out an arm, close to being hysterical. "Well, *do you*?"

In her mind's eye she could see the world: Dani and Blaise and all other witches on the left; Eric and ꟷꟷꟷꟷꟷts here and all other humans on the right, ꟷꟷꟷ races hating and despising each other—and herself somewhere in the middle.

Eric caught her shoulders. *"No, I don't think it's all right*. Thea, will you just *listen* to me for a second?"

He was almost shaking her—but she could see that there were tears forming at the corners of his eyes.

"I feel *awful*," he said. "I never thought about taking this stuff seriously—and that's my own stupid fault, and I know it's not an excuse. But now that you say it, I do see how terrible it is, and I'm sorry. And I never should have brought *you* here, of all people . . ."

Thea, who had been starting to relax, stiffened again. "Why me 'of all people'?" she demanded.

He hesitated a moment, then met her eyes and spoke quietly. "Because of your grandma's store. I mean, I know it's just herbs and positive thinking—but I also know that in the old days, there would have been somebody out there pointing a finger and calling her a witch."

Thea relaxed again. It was okay for people to think

Gran was a witch—if by "witch" they meant someone who talked to plants and mixed up homemade hair tonic. And she couldn't disbelieve Eric, not under the intensity of those steady green eyes.

But she saw an opportunity and seized it.

"Yeah, and they'd probably have burned *me* for giving you this present," she said, opening her hand. "And you'd probably have been scared or superstitious if I asked you to keep it with you all the time: you'd think I was putting some kind of a spell on you—"

"I wouldn't think anything," he said firmly, taking the little green pillow from her. It smelled like fresh New Hampshire pine needles, which was what was in it—mainly. She'd also added a few protective herbs and an Ishtar crystal, a golden beryl in a star cut with thirty-three facets, carved with the name of the Babylonian mother goddess. The charm was the best she could do to help him fend off Blaise's spells.

"I would just kiss it and put it my pocket and never let it out of my sight," Eric went on. And he did, stopping after the kiss to say, "Mm, smells good."

Thea couldn't help smiling at him. She chanced saying, "Actually, it's just to remind you of me."

"It will never leave my pocket," he said solemnly.

Well, that worked out nicely.

"Look, there's probably something we can do about this place," Eric said, glancing around again. "The school board doesn't want any bad publicity. Why don't I run and borrow a camera from the journalism class, and we can take some pictures so people will see what we mean when we complain?"

Thea glanced at her watch. "Why not? I think I've already missed French."

He grinned. "Back in a minute."

When he was gone, Thea wandered slowly among the silent booths, lost in her own thoughts.

For a few minutes there, when I was ranting, I almost told him the truth. And then later I thought maybe he'd figured it all out for himself.

And would that be so terrible? He's already under sentence of death just because I love him; it doesn't matter if he knows or not.

But if he did know . . . what would he say? Witches may be okay in the abstract—but does he really want one for a girlfriend?

The only way to find out was to tell him.

She leaned against a ladder and gazed sightlessly at an oilcloth lying beneath a hanging noose. Of course, it was probably all academic anyway. What kind of future could they possibly have . . . ?

Suddenly Thea realized what she was looking at.

Underneath that oilcloth was a shoe—and the shoe was connected to something. Subconsciously, she'd been assuming it was another witch dummy . . . but now she focused. And she felt the hairs on her arms lift and tingle.

Why would they dress a witch in black Nike high-tops?

CHAPTER

9

The shoe was so incongruous that for an instant Thea thought her eyes must be playing tricks on her. It was the atmosphere here—the dim, echoing room with all its macabre booths. If she looked away and then looked back . . .

It was still there.

I should wait, I should call somebody. This could be something terrible. There are human authorities; I should at least wait for Eric. . . .

Thea found herself moving in dreamlike, slow speed.

She took the edge of the oilcloth between finger and thumb and lifted it just an inch or so.

There was a leg attached to the shoe.

A blue-jeaned leg. Not part of a dummy. And another shoe.

Horror and adrenaline washed over Thea. And,

strangely, that helped. Her first thought was, *It's a person and she may be hurt*. She went into emergency mode, slamming a wall between herself and her fear.

Hang on, are you okay, just let me see . . .

She pulled the rest of the oilcloth off, tugging to get it free. She saw legs, a body, curled fingers clutching the sleeve of a black-dressed witch dummy . . .

Then she saw the head and she reeled backward, both hands pressed over her mouth. She'd only gotten a glimpse, but the picture was burned into her mind.

Blue-gray face, hideously swollen. Grotesquely bulging eyes. Tongue like a sausage protruding from between black lips . . .

Thea's knees gave out.

She'd seen the dead before. She'd been to leave-taking ceremonies where the mortal remains of witches were returned to the earth. But those had been natural deaths, and the corpses had been peaceful. While this . . .

I think it was a boy. It had short hair and a flat chest. But there was no way to recognize the face. It was so distorted—didn't even look human. . . .

He died violently. May his spirit be released; not held here by the need for revenge. Oh, Sekhmet, Lion-headed goddess of Egypt; Mistress of Death, Opener of Ways, Sekhmet Who Reduceth to Silence . . .

Her disjointed thoughts were interrupted as sunlight fanned into the room. At the door, Eric shouted, "I'm back!"

Thea stood up. Her legs wanted to cave again. She

opened her mouth, but what came out was a whisper. "Eric—"

He was hurrying toward her. "What's wrong? Thea?"

"It's somebody dead."

She saw his eyes widen in absolute disbelief—and then he looked past her. He took a step toward the thing on the floor, stopped, crouched, and stared for a second. Then he whirled back and grabbed her as if he could somehow protect her from what he'd seen.

"Don't look at it; don't look over there," he gasped. "Oh, God, it's bad."

"I know. I saw it."

"It's bad; it's so bad. . . ."

They were both holding on to each other. It was the only safety in this nightmare.

"He's dead. That guy is dead," Eric said. It was obvious, but Thea understood the need to babble. "There's nothing we can do for him. Oh, God, Thea, I think it's Kevin Imamura."

"*Kevin?*" Black dots danced in front of Thea's eyes. "No, it can't be—"

"I've seen him wearing that shirt before. And the hair . . . And he's on the committee to decorate this place. He must have been setting up that dummy."

Thea's mind showed her a terrible picture. A crusted dark line on that bloated face—like the wound made by a slashing razor. And the soft black hair . . . Yes, it could have been Kevin. And that meant—

Blaise.

"Come on," Eric was saying, his voice dazed and quenched. "We've got to tell the office."

Numbly, Thea let him guide her. Her mind was in another place.

Blaise. Did Blaise know . . . could Blaise have . . .

She didn't want to form the thought even to herself, but she couldn't help it.

. . . finally gone all the way? Not just spilled blood, but taken a life?

It was forbidden to witches. But the Harmans were part lamia, and vampires sometimes killed for power. Could Blaise have gone that far into the darkness?

After they got to the office, things happened fast, but Thea couldn't really take it in. Activity whirled around her. The secretaries. The principal. The police. She was grateful for Eric, who kept telling the story over and over so she didn't have to.

I need to find Blaise.

They were back at the gym. The police were cordoning off the whole building with yellow tape. A throng of students and teachers was watching. Thea's eyes skimmed the crowd, but she didn't see Blaise anywhere.

Voices rose around her.

"I heard it was Kevin Imamura."

"Somebody said that guy from the dance came back and got him."

"Eric! Eric, did you really *see* him?"

Then one voice outshouted the others. "Hey, Mrs. Cheng, what about the Halloween party? Is the gym gonna be open by then?"

The principal, who had been huddled with a couple of police officers, turned around. Black hair riffling over her forehead in the breeze, she addressed the entire crowd.

"I don't know what is going to happen with the gym. There's been a tragedy, and now there's going to be an investigation. We'll just have to wait and see what comes of that. Now, I want everybody to go back to their classes. Teachers, please take your students back to your classrooms."

"I can't go back," Thea whispered. She and Eric were standing at a little distance from the thinning crowd. Everyone seemed to have forgotten about them.

"I'll take you home," Eric said immediately.

"No—I need to find Blaise. I have some things to ask her." She tried to make her stupefied brain work. "Eric, I should have told you this before. You've got to be careful."

"Of what?"

"Of Blaise."

He looked incredulous. "Thea . . ." He glanced at the old gym. "You can't think *she* had anything to do with—what happened to Kevin."

"I don't know. She could have had somebody do it—or made him do it himself." Thea kept her voice low. She looked straight into Eric's face, willing him to believe her. "Eric, I know you don't understand, but it's like I told you before. She's like Aphrodite. Or Medea. She laughs when she destroys things. Especially when she gets mad . . . and she's mad at *you*."

"Why?"

"Because you picked me instead of her—because I like you—lots of things. *That* doesn't matter. The point is that she may come after you. She may try to . . . seduce you. And"—Thea glanced at the bobbing yellow tape surrounding the old gym—"she may try to hurt you. So will you just be *careful* if you see her? Will you promise me that?"

Eric looked windblown and bewildered, but he nodded slowly. "I promise."

"Then I'll see you later. We still have things to talk about—but I have to find Blaise first."

She walked toward the crowd, leaving Eric standing there in the wind. She knew he was watching her.

A waving hand caught Thea's eye. It was Dani, her face full of sympathy and concern.

"Thea, are you all right?"

"Sort of." Thea gave a laugh she didn't recognize. "Have you seen Blaise around?"

Dani's soft little hand crept into hers. "She and Vivienne went home—I mean, to your place. I'll go back with you, if you want. You shouldn't be alone."

Thea squeezed her hand. "Thanks. I'd appreciate it." She was grateful—and relieved that Dani didn't hate her. "Dani—about the way I acted earlier . . ."

"Forget it. I don't know what I said, but I didn't mean to make you mad." She added gently, "Thea, are you really okay? Really? Because I don't want to upset you more. . . ."

"Why?" And then: *"What*, Dani?"

"Your grandma's sick. That's why Blaise and Vivienne went home—Vivienne's mom paged her. She's a healer—Vivienne's mom, I mean—and I think she's taking your grandma to her house."

Thea was disturbed. Gran hadn't moved to Las Vegas for the same reason other Night People did. Lamia and made vampires came because so many of the humans here were transients—the kind that wouldn't be missed if they disappeared. Other witches came because of the power vortexes in the desert. But Gran had come because of the warm, dry climate. Her lungs had been bad since she was a kid.

Please don't let it be serious, Thea kept thinking as Dani drove her home. She felt as if her skin had been rubbed too thin all over her body.

When they got to the shop, Gran was already gone. Tobias and Vivienne were downstairs.

"Is she okay?" Thea asked. "Is it something bad?"

"Not too bad," Tobias said. "She just kept getting dizzy today, and then she had a coughing fit and couldn't stop. She finally decided maybe she'd better get somebody to sing it out. So she called Ms. Morrigan."

Oh, great—chanting. Just what Gran loved. But she must have been really sick to *ask* to have it done.

"Can I call her?"

"I wouldn't," Vivienne put in. Her green eyes were kind, her voice reassuring. "I'm sure Mom's working on her by now, and when she does a singing, it takes all night. You shouldn't disturb them. But don't worry, Thea—my mom's really good."

"Yes—it's not that I'm worried about." Thea looked around distractedly, finally coming back to Vivienne's face. "Did you hear about what happened at school?"

"No." Vivienne looked mildly curious. "*What* happened?"

Instead of answering, Thea said, "Where's Blaise?"

"Upstairs packing. She's going to stay overnight at my house. You can come, too—Thea?"

Thea was already racing up the stairs.

She burst into the bedroom she and Blaise shared. Blaise had a small suitcase open on her bed.

Thea didn't waste words. "Did you kill Kevin Imamura?"

Blaise dropped a black silk teddy. "Did I *what?* What are you talking about?"

"He's dead."

"And you thought *I* did it? Thanks a lot, but it's not him I want to kill." Blaise narrowed her eyes and Thea felt cold. Then she tilted her head. "So how did he die?"

"He was strangled. Somebody *murdered* him."

Blaise just raised her eyebrows and murmured, "Hm. I wonder where Randy is?" She held a shirt up, considered it, and added, "Do you want to come stay at Viv's with me? It's better than staying here by yourself."

"I don't know. Do I have to watch you to make sure *Eric* doesn't end up like Kevin?"

Blaise gave her a scorching look. "When I go after a boy, I *get* him first. I don't strangle him before the fun begins."

She slammed her suitcase closed and stalked out.

Thea sat on the bed.

In spite of her sharp words, Thea now knew Blaise hadn't done it. Her cousin had been genuinely surprised.

And Randy? *I suppose it could have been, if he somehow got out of wherever they've taken him. He had a reason to hate Kevin. But . . .*

The alternate explanation slid into place so quickly that Thea realized it must have been in her mind all along.

The spirit.

She sat there for an endless time, trying to think. It was like trying to find her way through a thick fog.

Gran's gone . . . and if she's sick I can't bother her anyway . . . of course, Blaise won't help . . . but I need to trust somebody. . . .

Dani gently pushed the door open. "Can I come in?" When Thea nodded, she walked in and sat down on Blaise's bed.

"They left. I told Tobias to go too—he had a girlfriend he wanted to see. I'll stay here tonight, if you want."

Thea took a shaky breath. "Thanks, Dani."

"Look, Thea, I don't want to pry, but . . . *are* you okay? I mean, you're as pale as a corpse—" Dani bit her lip. "Sorry, bad choice of words. But I *am* your friend, and if there's anything I can do, I'd like to help."

Another breath. Then Thea made her decision.

"I worked a forbidden spell."

Dani looked shocked, but not appalled. "Which one?"

"Calling back the spirits."

When Dani didn't scream or faint, Thea told the whole story. All about her summoning—everything except why she'd been doing it. "And now I'm scared," she finished. "I let *something* out yesterday, and today Kevin gets murdered. Blaise didn't kill him. She thinks Randy may be involved, but . . ." Thea shook her head.

"But, Thea, be logical. Why should it have anything to do with your spell?" Dani's rational voice was soothing. "You let some*one* out, not some*thing*. The elders summon the ancestors all the time without anything bad happening. You just feel guilty because you know you weren't *supposed* to be doing it."

"No. Dani, I can't explain it, but the thing I let out—it wasn't friendly. It knocked Blaise and me down. None of the spirits I saw the elders summon ever did that."

"Well . . ." Dani looked doubtful. "But why would one of the ancestors went to murder a human?"

"I don't know." Somehow talking about it had cleared Thea's mind. She said slowly, "But . . . maybe the book would tell us."

Ten minutes later, they were sitting side by side on Thea's bed, with the iron chest on the floor and the book between them.

"First, could you tell *anything* about the amulet that fell in the fire?" Dani asked in scientific tones. "Like, if the hair was gray, it could mean—"

"The witch was old." Thea caught on immediately. "No, it wasn't gray or white. It was dark—sort of like mahogany." She closed her eyes, trying to remember.

"It all happened so fast—but I think it was *long*. It was doubled up lots of times in the clay."

"So maybe a woman."

"Yes." Thea read for several minutes. "Wait a minute. Look at this."

" 'Suzanne Blanchet,' " Dani read with difficulty. " 'Born sixteen thirty-four in Esgavans on the day that they made bonfires for the peace between France and Spain. Tried sixteen fifty-three at Ronchain, prisoner at the court of Rieux.' "

"And listen to the charges," Thea said grimly. " 'Bewitching men's corn, killing cattle, bringing hunger into the country, *and strangling babies at night with her long hair.*' "

"Strangling," Dani breathed.

"She denied it, so they tortured her. Listen: 'Being a little stretched on the rack, she screamed ceaselessly that she was not a witch, but being more tightly stretched, said that it was true.' "

"And then they tortured her *family*," Dani said, her finger skimming the lines. "Oh, Isis, look at this. She had a ten-year-old brother named Clément and a six-year-old sister named Lucienne. They tortured them both."

"And burned them." Thea had begun to tremble involuntarily. The room wasn't cold, but she had a feeling like ice deep inside her. "Look. 'The children having been promised the mercy of being strangled before burning, but the executioner not having been paid, they were committed alive to the flames . . .' " She couldn't finish.

" '. . . before the eyes of their sister,' " Dani whispered. She was shaking, too, and huddling close to Thea. "How could they *do* that?"

"I don't know," Thea said flatly.

"I mean, no wonder Night World laws are so strict. No wonder we have to keep ourselves a secret—look at what they *do* to us when they find out."

Thea swallowed—she didn't want to think about Night World rules. "And then they burned Suzanne," she said quietly, keeping her eyes on the book. " 'Being consigned to the fire, she uttered several exclamations, crying out upon revenge.' "

"I would too," Dani said, her soft voice threaded with steel. "I'd come back and *kill* them."

She stopped and she and Thea looked at each other.

"And maybe that's just what she did," Thea said slowly. "Only she couldn't get to her torturers. But she found something that looked similar—a reproduction torture chamber. And there was Kevin, doing something to a witch dummy—hanging it, maybe. Maybe treating it in some way that reminded her of . . ." Thea nodded toward the book. "Anyway, doing *something* that made her lose it."

"And kill him. By strangling him—what she'd been accused of doing. Thea?" Dani grimaced, then went on. "When you saw Kevin's body—was there anything around his neck?"

Thea stared at the window curtains, trying to remember. That awful bloated face . . . the protruding tongue . . . and dark bruises on the throat.

"No," she said softly. "There were marks—but whatever strangled him was gone."

"She took it with her." Dani shivered, then put both hands on the book. "Or maybe not. Look, Thea, this may make a great bonfire story, but, really, it's all speculation."

Thea was staring at the yellowed page beneath Dani's fingers. "I don't think so," she said quietly. "See this symbol by Suzanne Blanchet's name? I recognize it. I saw it for just a second—on the amulet in the fire."

"You're sure?"

Thea looked away. "Yeah. It's her, Dani. And it's my fault. I let her out . . . and now she's killing people. Because of me, somebody's *dead*."

It was only when she said it that the full realization hit—as if forming the words had somehow made it true. Kevin was *dead*. He wasn't going to school anymore, he wasn't going to get a chance to repair his Porsche. He wouldn't ever smile at a girl again. He'd lost everything a person had to lose.

"And I just—I just feel so *bad*," Thea said. The ache in her throat rose up in a sort of spasm, as if she were going to be sick. But what came out was tears.

Dani held her while she sobbed. And at last, when Thea was crying more quietly, she said, "You didn't know. You didn't mean to do anything bad. You were just playing around and it went wrong. *You didn't know.*"

"It doesn't matter." Thea wiped her face on her sleeve, sitting up. The ache in her chest was duller now, and she was slowly realizing that something else was there, something that felt hot and bright. A need to *act*.

"It doesn't matter," she said again. "I still made it happen. But I'll tell you one thing—I'm not going to let it *keep* happening. I've got to stop her. Which means I've got to send her back."

"I'm with you there," Dani said, her small jaw set in determination. "But *how?*"

Thea stared at the wall a moment, then said, "I have an idea."

CHAPTER

10

ran told me that the only person who can send a spirit back is the one who called it up," Thea said. "But the problem is that you have to be able to *see* the spirit, you have to be close to it. Then you can do the sending-back spell."

"Okay," Dani said, nodding. "But—"

"Wait, I'm getting to it." Thea got up and began to pace the few steps between her bed and Blaise's. She spoke slowly at first, then more rapidly. "What I'm thinking is that this can't be the first time this has happened. Sometime, somewhere, somehow, some witch must have called up a spirit and let it get away. And then had to go out and get hold of it again."

"I'm sure that's true. But so what?"

"So if we could find a record of how she did it— how she tracked the spirit down—we might be in business."

Dani was getting excited. "Yeah—and it wouldn't even have to be a case of a *summoned* spirit. I mean, some spirits just won't go to the other side at all after they've died, right? Maybe there's a record about how one of *them* got sent across the veil."

"Or a story. Or a poem. *Anything* that would give us a clue about how to get them to stay in the same room with you while you do the spell." Thea stopped and grinned at Dani. "And if there's one thing Gran has lots of, it's records and stories and poems. There are hundreds of books in the workshop."

Dani jumped up, dark eyes snapping. "I'll call my mom and tell her I'm staying over tonight. Then— we find it."

After Dani called her mother, Thea called Eric to make sure he was okay. Now that she knew there was a demented spirit on the loose she was worried about him.

"You're sure *you're* all right?" he said. "I mean, I still feel awful about taking you to that place. I wanted—well, I'd like it if we could see each other *without* something terrible happening."

Thea felt as if someone had squeezed her heart. "Me, too."

"Maybe we could do something tomorrow. If you're up to it."

"That would be good." She didn't dare to keep talking to him with Dani around. It would be too easy for anyone listening to guess her feelings.

The first thing Thea noticed in the workshop was that Blaise had taken her new project with her.

She must be close to finishing it.

"I'll start here," Dani said, standing in front of a large bookcase. "Some of these look really old."

Thea picked another case. There were books of every kind: leather-bound, paper-bound, cloth-bound, suede-bound, unbound. Some were printed, some were handwritten, some were illuminated. Some were in languages Thea didn't know.

The first shelf yielded nothing except an interesting spell titled "HOW TO MAKE AN ELIXIR OF ABHORRENCE, which works quite as well, or perhaps a little worse than the traditional Elixirs of Loathing or Detestation, and is less delicate and expensive than the Elixir of Odium used by royals and members of the nobility, and will also keep extremely well for a very long time."

Hmm . . .

Thea put that book aside. She'd looked through another half a shelf when Dani said, "Hey, I found your family tree."

Thea scooted over. "Yeah, that's the one Gran keeps. It doesn't go anywhere near back to Helle-wise." She laughed.

"Who's this guy?" Dani put her finger on a name. " 'Hunter Redfern.' I thought the Redferns were that hotshot vampire family."

"Lamia family. I mean, there's a difference, you know. Someone who's *made* into a vampire can't have kids."

"But what's the lamia guy doing in your family tree?"

"He's the one who did a kinship ceremony with

Maeve Harman, back in the sixteen hundreds. She was the leader of the Harmans then. See? And we're all descended from their daughter Roseclear."

"She did it with a *vampire?* Creepy."

Thea smiled. "She did it to stop their families from fighting—they had a feud going on. And so now all of us modern Harmans have a little vampire blood."

"I'll remember to watch out if you start looking at my throat." Dani traced a finger down the tree. "It looks like you and Blaise are the last of the female Harmans."

"Yeah, we're it. The last Hearth-Women."

"That's a big responsibility."

It was almost exactly what Gran had said. Thea suddenly felt uncomfortable with family trees. "Yeah. Um, I guess we'd better keep reading."

It was several hours later when Dani said quietly, "I've got it."

"What?" Thea went to sit by her. The book on Dani's knees was bound in green with a crescent moon and three stars on the front—a Night World symbol for witches.

"It's a book of humorous stories, but they're supposed to be true. This one is about a guy named Walstan Harman back in seventeen seventy. He died, but he didn't cross over. He just hung around town playing jokes on everybody—appearing at night with his head under his arm and stuff like that. He never stayed in one place long enough for them to catch him, though."

"So how did they track him down?"

Dani flashed a triumphant smile. "They didn't. They *lured* him *in*."

Light dawned for Thea. "Of course—I'm so stupid. But *how?*"

Dani's slender finger swept down the page. "Well, first they waited till Samhain, so the veil between the worlds would be thinnest. Then Nicholas Harman had this big feast prepared, this huge table piled up with Walstan's favorite food." Dani made a face. "Which happened to be mince pie made with bear meat and pumpkin, with a cornmeal crust. They have a recipe for it here, too. Gah."

"Never mind that. Did it work?"

"Apparently. They set up the table with the pies in an empty room, then they cast a circle around it. Old Walstan was attracted to the food—I guess he just couldn't resist taking a look, even if he couldn't eat it. And when he came down to check it out, they opened the door and nabbed him."

" 'Sent him speedily and conveniently through the narrow path to the airy void,' " Thea read over Dani's shoulder. The story sounded genuine—only someone who'd actually seen a summoning or a sending-back would know those words.

"So now we know how to do it," Dani said. "We wait until Halloween and then we *lure* her. We just have to find something she likes—"

"Or . . . something she *hates*," Thea broke in as an idea struck her.

They stared at each other.

"Like what she saw at the old gym," Dani

breathed. "Something that reminded her of what they did to her."

"Yes, except . . ." Thea stopped. Her mind was racing on, but she didn't want to share her thoughts with Dani. Except that the humans might already be doing something on Halloween, something that would attract Suzanne. If the police opened the old gym, the Halloween party would be an incredibly strong lure. All those horror booths . . .

So if I wanted to draw her somewhere else, I'd need to be doing something even *worse*, something that would remind her even more of what happened to her. And I'd need bait, somebody she'd want to kill. A human. Somebody who'd work with me, who'd be willing . . .

Not Eric.

Her thoughts came up short as she realized where they were leading. She found that her hands were icy cold and her heart was pounding slowly.

No. Not Eric, no matter what. Not even to save lives.

She pushed the thought from her mind. Of course there was some other way, and she'd find it. There was time. . . .

"Thea? You still with me?" Dani was watching her.

"I was just trying to figure it all out." Thea forced herself to speak calmly, to focus on Dani. "Um, listen, there's one good thing I just thought of—we may have a little time. If Suzanne is *still* watching the old gym, it could work for us. As long as the gym is closed up, people won't go in there, and she won't be able to get anybody."

"I hope so," Dani said. "I mean, I understand why she's upset, but nobody deserves to die the way Kevin did. Not even a human."

Late that night, while Dani was breathing peacefully in Blaise's bed, Thea lay and stared at the faint glow above the window curtains.

It wasn't just visions of Kevin. Her mind kept returning to what Dani and Gran had said about her responsibility.

Even if I send Suzanne back, even if Gran gets well, even if I manage to keep Blaise from killing Eric . . . where am I?

I'm a renegade witch. And there's no future for Eric and me . . . unless we run away. But that would mean him leaving his family forever—and us being hunted wherever we went. And me betraying the Hearth-Women and the Night World.

One last thought glimmered before she could force her mind into blankness.

There's no way everybody is going to come out of this happy.

The next morning Thea was late for school. And she had a hard time tracking down Blaise—it wasn't until lunchtime that she and Dani found the Circle Midnight witches in the front courtyard.

"Please let us see it," Selene was saying as Thea and Dani walked up. "Just one peek. Please?"

"I want to do a trial run first," Blaise said, looking very pleased with herself. She took a drink of iced tea, ignoring Thea and Dani.

"How's Gran?" Thea broke in without preamble.

Blaise turned. "Better, no thanks to you. Why didn't you call this morning?"

"I overslept." After terrible nightmares about strangled people.

"We were up late last night," Dani said. "It's not Thea's fault."

"Your grandma's really doing well," Vivienne said kindly. "She just needs to rest for a while—Mom'll probably keep her at our place for a couple of days. Sleep heals, you know."

Thea felt a tiny breath of relief, like a spring breeze. If Gran was getting better she had one less thing to worry about. "Thanks, Viv. Please thank your mom, too."

Blaise raised her eyebrows and made a tiny sound like "Hmf." Then she tapped her chin with one long nail. "A trial run . . ." she said again, gazing far away.

She was dressed unusually, in a bronze silk jacket with a high collar that was zipped up to her chin. Thea had a sudden sinking feeling.

"What are you trying out?" Dani asked.

Blaise gave them a slow smile. "Hang around and you'll see." She scanned the courtyard and said sweetly, "And *there* is the perfect mark. Selene, will you go ask him to come here?"

Selene got up and languidly drifted to the boy Blaise had pointed at.

Thea recognized him. He was Luke Price, a guy who drove a sleek red Maserati and looked like a bad-boy Hollywood star. He was fashionably un-shaven and unkempt, had electric blue eyes, and right now looked vaguely surprised to find himself following Selene back to Blaise.

"Luke, how's it going?" Blaise said pleasantly.

Luke shrugged. "Okay. What do you want?" His electric blue eyes lingered on Blaise, but he was obviously used to playing the tough guy with girls.

Blaise laughed shortly, as if taken off guard by the question. "Nothing I can have," she murmured—and then looked slightly startled at herself. "I want to talk to you," she said smoothly, recovering. "And . . ." She tilted her head thoughtfully. "Maybe the keys to your car."

Luke laughed out loud. He leaned one hip against the concrete wall by the stairs, two fingers fishing in his T-shirt pocket for a cigarette.

"You're crazy," he said indistinctly.

Dani coughed as smoke drifted toward her. Thea swirled her plastic bottle of Evian water in one hand.

Blaise made a face. "Put that out; it's disgusting," she said.

Luke blew smoke toward her. "If you've got something to say, say it." He was eyeing Blaise's zipped-to-the-neck jacket with disfavor. "Otherwise stop wasting my time."

Blaise smiled.

She touched the zipper at her throat. "You want to guess what's under here?"

Luke's eyes went up and down the silk of the jacket, particularly where Blaise made it curve. "Maybe you'd better show me."

"You want me to show you? You're *sure*, now?"

Thea looked heavenward, thumb playing with the opening to her Evian bottle.

Luke was scowling, blowing smoke between tight lips. His electric blue eyes were narrow. "I think you're some kind of tease. . . ."

Blaise took the zipper between two fingers and slid it down.

The necklace fit like a collar, lying against the pale skin of her throat and the matte black of her simple blouse. And it was everything Thea had known it would be.

It was delicate, exquisite, magical. Swirls of stars and moons in enchanted patterns. Gems of all kinds tucked into the mysterious curves. Green garnet, imperial topaz, sunstone, cinnabar. Violet sapphire, African emerald, smokestone.

It seemed to move as you looked at it, the lines changing and flowing. Pulling you into the center of its mystery, winding around you like strands of softly burnished hair. Holding you fast . . .

Thea pulled herself away with a physical jerk. She had to shut her eyes and put up a hand to do it.

And if it does that to *me* . . .

Luke was staring. Thea could actually *see* the change in his face as the necklace worked its spell. Like some Oscar-winning actor transforming from bad boy to vulnerable kid right there on screen. His jaw softened, his tight lips relaxed. The muscles around his eyes shifted and he lost his tense squint. He looked surprised, then defenseless. Open. Those electric blue eyes seemed dazzled, pupils widening. He sucked in a breath as if he couldn't get enough air. Now he looked awed; now hypnotized; now yearning . . .

Spellbound.

Luke had been transformed. His whole body seemed smaller. His lips were parted. His eyes were huge and full of light. He looked as if at any second he might fall down and start worshiping Blaise.

Blaise sat like a queen, with her midnight hair tumbling around the necklace, her chest moving slightly as she breathed, her eyes as brilliant as jewels.

"Put the disgusting cigarette down," she said.

Luke dropped the cigarette and stamped on it as if it were a spider.

Then he looked back at Blaise. "You . . . you're beautiful." He reached a hand toward her.

"Wait," Blaise said. Her face assumed a tragic, wistful expression. "First, I'm going to tell you a sad story. I used to have a little dog that I loved, a cocker spaniel, and we would take long walks together around dusk."

Thea gave her cousin a narrow sideways look. She'd never heard such a lie. And what was Blaise talking about *dogs* for?

"But he was run over by an eighteen-wheel Piggly Wiggly truck," Blaise murmured. "And ever since, I've been so lonely. . . . I miss him so much." She fixed her eyes on the boy in front of her. "Luke . . . will you be my little dog?"

Luke looked confused.

"You see," Blaise went on, slipping a hand in her pocket, "if I could just have somebody to remind me of him, I'd feel so much better. So if you'd wear this for me . . ."

She was holding a blue dog collar.

Luke looked even more confused. Redness was creeping up his neck and jaw. His eyes filled.

"For me?" Blaise coaxed, jingling the collar—which was way too big for a spaniel, Thea noticed. "I'd be *so* grateful."

Luke looked as if he were having a tremendous internal struggle. His breathing was uneven. He swallowed. A muscle in his jaw twitched.

Then, very slowly, he reached for the collar. Blaise held it down low.

Luke's eyes followed the collar. Jerkily, as if his muscles were fighting each other, he knelt down at Blaise's side. He stayed there, stone-faced, as Blaise fastened the dog collar around his neck.

When it was secure, Blaise laughed. She glanced at the other girls, then jingled the metal loop for the dog tag. "Good boy," she said, and patted his head.

Luke's face lit up with an excitement that bordered on ecstasy. He stared into Blaise's eyes.

"I love you," he said huskily, still squatting.

Blaise wrinkled her nose and laughed again. Then she zipped up the bronze jacket.

The change on Luke's face was much quicker this time than his first transformation. For an instant he looked completely blank, then he glanced around as if he'd suddenly woken up in a classroom.

His fingers went to the dog collar. His face contracted in anger and horror and he jumped up.

"What's going on? What am I doing?"

Blaise just gazed at him serenely.

Luke tore the collar off and kicked it. Although he was glaring at Blaise, he didn't seem to remember the last few minutes. "You—are you gonna tell me what you want or not?" he snapped, his upper lip trembling. "Because I'm not going to wait all day."

Then, when nobody said anything, he walked huffily off. His buddies across the courtyard were roaring with laughter.

"Oops," Blaise said. "I forgot about the car keys." She turned to the other girls. "But I'd say it works."

"I'd say it's *scary*," Dani whispered.

"I'd say it's incredible," Selene murmured.

"I'd say it's unbelievable," Vivienne added.

And *I'd* say it's the Armageddon of accessories, Thea thought. And, incidentally, so much for Selene and Vivienne changing their ways. They may have been shocked at what happened to Randy and Kevin, but it sure didn't last.

"Blaise," she said tightly, "if you walk around school showing that, you are going to cause a riot."

"But I'm not *going* to walk around school showing it," Blaise said. "There's only one guy I'm interested in right now. And this"—she touched her throat—"has *his* blood in it. If it works like that on other people, I wonder what it will do to him?"

Thea took a few deep breaths to relax her stomach. She had never gone one-on-one with Blaise in a matter of witchcraft. And no one had ever challenged Blaise for a boy.

But she didn't have a choice—and putting this off wouldn't help.

"I suppose you're planning to find some time to ambush him," she said. "Some time when I'm not around."

It worked. Blaise stood, tall and regal in her bronze silk jacket, hands in her pockets, hair like a waterfall behind her. She gave Thea a slow smile.

"I don't need to ambush anybody," she said with dreadful confidence. "In fact . . . why don't we set up a meeting after school? Just the three of us. You, me, and Eric—a showdown. And may the best witch win."

CHAPTER

11

I don't understand," Eric said pitifully as Thea towed him toward the bleachers.

"Well, that's reasonable."

"Blaise wants to talk to me alone and you want me to *do* it."

"That's right." Thea hadn't realized it was possible to sound bright and bleak at the same time. "I told you she'd probably go after you—"

"And you told me to be careful of her. You made the point very strongly."

"I know. It's just . . ." Thea searched for an explanation that wouldn't be too much of a lie and clutched her bottle of Evian water. She didn't need to ask him if he had the protective charm with him— she could smell New Hampshire pine needles.

"It's just that I think it's better to get things settled," she said finally. "One way or the other. So maybe if you talk to her face-to-face . . . well, you can decide what you want, and we can get this over with.''

"Thea . . .'' Eric stopped, forcing Thea to stop, too. He looked completely bewildered. "Thea—I don't know what you're thinking, but I don't *need* to talk to Blaise to know what I want.'' He put his hands gently on her upper arms. "Nothing she can say could make any difference.''

Thea looked at him, at his clean, good features and his expressive eyes. He thought things were so simple.

"Then you can just tell her that,'' she said, trying to sound optimistic. "And the whole thing will be resolved.''

Eric shook his head, but allowed her to guide him onward.

Blaise was leaning against a concrete dugout by the baseball diamond. When they were about ten feet away, Thea stopped and nodded at Eric to keep going.

He walked to Blaise, who slowly straightened with the leisurely grace of a snake uncoiling.

Thea put her thumb into the Evian bottle and jiggled it gently.

"Thea said you wanted to talk to me.'' Eric's voice was polite, but not encouraging. He looked back at Thea after he said it.

"I did,'' Blaise said in her liquid, persuasive voice. But to Thea's surprise, she addressed the ground, as if she felt awkward. "But now . . . well, I feel so embarrassed. I know what you probably think of

me—trying to say something like this while your girlfriend is standing there."

"Well . . ." Eric glanced back at Thea again. "It's
okay," he added, his voice softer. "I mean, it's better
to say whatever it is in front of her than behind
her back."

"Yes. Yes, that's true." Blaise took a deep breath
as if steeling herself and then lifted her head to meet
Eric's eyes.

What on *earth* is she doing? Thea stared at her
cousin. Where did this scene come from?

"Eric . . . I don't know how to say this, but . . . I
care about you. I know how that sounds. You're
thinking that I have dozens of guys, and the way I
treat them I can't possibly care about any of them.
And I don't blame you if you just want to walk away
right now, without even listening to any more."
Blaise fiddled with the zipper at her throat.

"Oh, look, I'm not going to walk away. I wouldn't
do that to you," Eric said, and his voice was even
more gentle.

"Thank you. You're being so nice—much nicer
than I deserve."

Absently, as if it were the most casual of gestures,
Blaise reached for the zipper at her throat and pulled
it down.

The necklace was revealed.

Don't look directly at it, Thea told herself. She stared
instead at the back of Eric's sandy head—which suddenly went very still.

"And you know, this is going to sound strange,
but most of those boys don't really like me." Blaise's

voice was soft now—seductive but vulnerable. "They just—want me. They look at the surface, and never even try to see any deeper. And that makes me feel . . . so lonely sometimes."

In Thea's peripheral vision, gold stars and moons were shifting and flowing. Yemonja root and other delicious scents wafted toward her. She hadn't even noticed that the first time; she'd been too deep in the necklace's spell to analyze it. And a faint, high resonance hung in the air—two or three notes that seemed to shimmer almost above the threshold of hearing.

Singing crystals. Of course. Blaise was assaulting every sense, weaving an inescapable golden web . . . and the whole thing was tuned to Eric's blood.

"All I've ever wanted is a guy who cares enough about me to look deeper than the surface." Blaise's voice had a slight catch now. "And—well, before I knew Thea liked you, I guess I thought you might be that guy. Eric, please tell me—is that completely impossible? Should I just totally give up hope? Because if you say so, I will."

Eric was standing oddly now, as if he were crippled. Thea could see his breath coming faster. She didn't want to see his face—she knew what it would be like. Like Luke's. Blank wonder changing into slow adulation for Blaise.

"Just tell me," Blaise said, raising one hand in a gesture full of pathos. "And if you say no, I'll go away forever. But if . . . if you think you could care about me . . . even just a little . . ." She gazed at him with luminous, yearning eyes.

"I . . ." Eric's voice was thick and hesitant. "I . . . Blaise . . ." He couldn't seem to get started on a sentence.

And no wonder. He's lost already.

Certainty hit Thea, and she stopped shaking her plastic bottle. Her little Elixir of Abhorrence didn't stand a chance against Blaise's magic. Eric was hooked and Blaise was reeling him in.

And it wasn't his fault. Nobody could be expected to hold out against the kind of enchantment Blaise was using. Enchantment and psychology so beautifully mixed that even Thea found herself half believing Blaise's story.

But she had to try anyway. She couldn't let Eric go without a fight.

With one final, violent shake, Thea took her thumb out of the bottle neck. Colorless liquid skyrocketed, spraying up and then raining down on Eric. A geyser of loathing.

Only one thing went wrong. As soon as the mysterious downpour hit Eric, he turned to see where it was coming from. Instead of looking at Blaise when the elixir soaked into his skin, he was looking at Thea.

She stared back into his gray-flecked eyes with a kind of horror.

Twice. He'd been twice enchanted now, once to love Blaise and once to hate *her*.

Oh, Eileithyia, it's over. . . .

It was a crisis, and Thea responded instinctively. She reached for Eric, to save him, to be saved herself.

She flung out a thought the way she'd fling out a hand to someone going over a cliff.

Eric.

A connection . . .

Like closing a circuit—and that was all it took. Thea felt a wave of . . . *something,* something hot and sweet, more magical than Blaise's magic. Distilled lightning, maybe. The air between her and Eric was so charged that she felt as though her skin was being brushed with velvet. It was like being at the intersection of cosmic force lines.

And it was all okay. Eric's face was his ordinary face. Alive, alert, full of warmth—for her. Not zombie worship for Blaise.

Thea.

It can't be this simple.

But it was. She and Eric were staring at each other in the quivering air and the universe was just one big singing crystal.

We're right together.

A yell shattered the silent communion. Thea looked toward the dugout and saw that Blaise the vulnerable had disappeared.

"I'm *wet,*" Blaise shrieked. "Are you crazy? Do you have any *idea* what water drops do to silk?"

Thea opened her mouth, then shut it again. She felt giddy with the sweetness of relief. She had no idea if Blaise really thought the elixir was only water—but one thing was clear. However strong Blaise's spell had been, it was broken now. And Blaise knew it.

Blaise jerked the zipper up and stalked off.

"She's mad," Eric said.

"Well . . ." Thea was still dizzy. "I told you she likes getting mad." She took Eric's arm, very gently, and partly to steady herself. "Let's go."

They'd only gone a few steps when Eric said, "Thank God you hit me with that water."

"Yes." Even if the elixir hadn't worked it had somehow broken Eric's concentration or distracted Blaise or something. She'd have to see if she could figure out what had happened to disrupt a spell as potent as the one Blaise had created. . . .

"Yeah, because, you know, it was getting really awkward," Eric went on. "I kept trying to think of a polite way to tell her there wasn't a chance, but I couldn't. And just when I realized I was going to have to *say* it and hurt her feelings—well, you soaked us."

Thea stopped dead. She stared at him.

He was serious.

"I mean—I know I hurt her feelings anyway. Or she wouldn't have gone away mad. Uh, are *you* mad now? Thea?"

She started walking again. "Are you saying you didn't even *want* to be with her? Not even just a little?"

He stopped. "How could I want to be with her when I want to be with you? I told you that before this whole thing started."

Maybe it's because we're soulmates. Maybe it's because he's so *stubborn*. But, whatever, I'd better never tell Blaise. She'll have a whole new reason for killing him if she finds out her spell bounced off like water off a duck.

"Well, anyway, it's resolved now," she murmured—and at that moment she really believed it. She was too happy to think about anything dreadful.

"Is it? Does that mean that we can finally go out? Like on a date?"

He sounded so wistful that Thea laughed. She felt light and free and full of energy. "Yeah. We could go right now. Or . . . we could go *in*. Your house, I mean. I'd like to see your sister and Madame Curie again."

Eric made an "ouch" face. "Well, Madame Curie would probably like that. But Roz lost her case— the court ruled that the Boy Trekkers are a private organization. And she is not—pardon the pun—a happy camper."

"All the more reason we should go see her. Poor kid."

Eric looked at her quizzically. "You're serious? You have a choice of anywhere in Las Vegas and you'd like to go to *my house*?"

"Why not?" Thea didn't mention that a human house was more exotic to her than anywhere else in Vegas.

She was happy.

It turned out to be a modest frame house, shaded by a couple of honest-to-goodness trees, not palms. Thea felt a twinge of shyness as they went inside.

"Mom's still at work. And"—Eric checked his watch—"Roz is supposed to be in her room until five.

Home detention. This morning she microwaved her Barbie dolls."

"That doesn't sound good for the microwave."

Rosamund's door was plastered with homemade signs. DO NOT ENTER. KEEP OUT AND THIS MEANS ERIC. FEMINISM IS THE RADICAL NOTION THAT WOMEN ARE PEOPLE.

When Eric opened the door a piggy bank shaped like a skunk came flying toward him. He ducked. It hit the wall and, amazingly, didn't break.

"Roz—"

"I hate everybody! And everybody hates me!" A hardback book came soaring.

Eric shut the door fast. *Bang.*

"Everybody doesn't hate you!" he yelled.

"Well, I hate them! *Go away!*"

Bang. Bang. *Crash.*

"I think maybe we'd better leave her alone," Eric said. "She gets a little moody sometimes. Want to see *my* room?"

His room was nice, Thea decided. Lots of books, some smelling of mildew—"I get them at the used book stores." *Comparative Vertebrate Anatomy. Development and Structure of the Fetal Pig. The Red Pony.* Most of them were about animals in some form or other.

And lots of trophies. Baseball trophies, basketball trophies, a few tennis trophies. "I have to switch between baseball and tennis different years." Sports equipment was scattered carelessly around, mixed with the books and some dirty socks.

Not so different from a teenager's room in the Night World. Just a *person's* room.

There was a picture of a man on the desk, a man

with sandy hair and a glorious, lightning-bolt smile like Eric's.

"Who is it?"

"My dad. He died when Roz was little—a plane crash. He was a pilot." Eric said it simply, but his eyes went dark.

Thea said softly, "My parents died when I was little, too. What's sad is that I don't really remember them."

Eric looked at the picture again. "You know, I never thought about it, but I'm glad I *do* remember. At least we had him that long."

They smiled at each other.

By the bed was a tank that gave off a pleasant percolating sound. Thea sat next to it and watched iridescent blue fish dart around. She turned off the bedside lamp to see the lighted tank better.

"You like it?"

"I like everything," Thea said. She looked at him. "Everything."

Eric blinked. He eyed the bed Thea was sitting on, then slowly sat at the desk. He stuck out a casual elbow to lean on and papers showered to the floor.

"Oops."

Thea stifled a laugh. "Is that the U.C. Davis application?"

He looked up hopefully from gathering them. "It sure is. Want to see it?"

Thea almost said yes. She was in such a cheerful mood, ready to agree to anything, be open to anything. But a moment of thought changed her mind. Some things were just going too far.

"Not right now, thanks."

"Well . . ." He put the papers back. "You know, you still might think about transferring to the zoology class at school. Ms. Gasparro is a great teacher. And you'd really like what we're studying."

Maybe I could, Thea thought. What would it hurt?

"And if you were ever interested, Dr. Salinger is always looking for extra help. It doesn't pay much, but it's good experience."

And . . . what would *that* hurt? It's not as if I would be breaking any laws. I wouldn't have to use any powers, either, I could just be close to the animals.

"I'll think about it," she said. She could hear the suppressed excitement in her own voice. She looked at Eric, who was sitting with his elbows on his knees, leaning forward, watching her earnestly. "And— thanks," she said softly.

"For what?"

"For . . . wanting the best for me. For caring."

The light from the fish tank threw wavering blue patterns on the walls and ceiling. It made the bed- room seem like its own little underwater world. It danced over Thea's skin.

Eric stared at her. Then he swallowed and shut his eyes. With his eyes still shut, he said in a muted voice, "I don't think you know how *much* I care."

Then he looked at her.

That connection again. It seemed to be drawing them together—an almost physical feeling of at- traction. It was exciting, but scary.

Eric got up very slowly and crossed the room. He sat by Thea. Neither of them looked away.

And *then* things just seemed to happen by themselves. Their fingers were intertwined. Thea was looking up and he was looking down. They were so close that their breath mingled. Thea shivered with the electricity.

Everything seemed wrapped in a golden haze.

Crash.

Something hit the other side of the wall.

"Ignore it; it's poltergeists," Eric murmured. His lips were an inch from hers.

"It's Rosamund," Thea murmured back. "She feels bad—and it's not really fair. We should try and make her feel better." She was so happy that she wanted everyone else to be happy, too.

Eric groaned. "Thea . . ."

"Let me just go see if I can cheer her up. I'll come back."

Eric shut his eyes, opened them, and turned on the lamp. He gave her a pained smile. "Okay. I have to water Mom's outside plants and feed the rabbits and stuff, anyway. Let me know when she's cheered up enough. I'll be waiting."

Thea knocked and ducked as she entered Rosamund's room. "Roz? Can I just talk to you for a minute?"

"Don't call me that. I want you to call me Fred."

"Uh, how come Fred?" Thea sat cautiously on the edge of the bed—or not the bed, actually, the box springs. The mattress was across the room, standing on its side in a corner. The entire room looked as if it had been hit simultaneously by a hurricane and an earthquake, and it smelled strongly of guinea pig.

Slowly, part of a sandy head appeared above the mattress. One green eye regarded Thea directly.

"Because," Rosamund said with terrible maturity, "I'm not a girl anymore. Things have always been this way for girls and they will always be this way and they are never going to change. And don't give me any of that B.S. about how females hear better and do better in submarines and have better fine motor skills, because *I don't care*. I'm going to be a boy now."

"You're a smart kid," Thea said. She was surprised at how smart Roz was, and at how much she wanted to comfort her. "But you need to study your history. Things *haven't* always been this way. There were times when women and men were equals."

Rosamund just said, "When?"

"Well—in ancient Crete, for one thing. They were all children of Eileithyia, the Great Goddess, and boys and girls both did dangerous stuff, like acrobatics on wild bulls. Of course . . ." Thea paused, struck by a thought. "The Greeks did come and conquer them."

"Uh-huh."

"But, um"—Thea wracked her brain for human history—"Well, the ancient Celts were okay—until the Romans came and conquered *them*. And . . . and . . ."

Human history was a problem.

"I told you," Rosamund said bitterly. "It always turns out the same. Now go away."

"Well . . ." Thea hesitated.

It was the excitement that did it. The giddy feeling of everything being right with the world. It made her overconfident, made her feel as if Night World law were a little thing that could be dispensed with if necessary.

Don't, a part of her mind whispered. *Don't or you'll be sorry.*

But Rosamund was so miserable. And the golden glow was still around Thea, making her feel protected. Invulnerable.

"Look," she said. "This may not help much, but I'll tell you a story, a story that always made me feel better when I was a little girl. Only you have to keep it a secret."

There was a flicker of interest in Rosamund's green eyes. "A true story?"

"Well—I can't really say it's true." And *that's* true—I *can't*. "But it's a good story, and it's about a time when women were leaders. About a girl called Hellewise."

CHAPTER

12

Thea settled on the box springs, not the most comfortable seat. "Now, this all happened back in the days when there was still magic, okay? And Hellewise could do magic, and so could most of the people in her tribe. She was the daughter of Hecate Witch-Queen—"

"She was a witch?" Roz sounded intrigued.

"Well—they didn't call it that then. They called her a Hearth-Woman. And she didn't look like a Halloween witch. She was beautiful: tall, with long yellow hair—"

"Like you."

"Huh? Oh." Thea grinned. "Thanks, but, no. Hellewise was *really* beautiful—and she was smart and strong, too. And when Hecate died, Hellewise became co-leader of the tribe. The other leader was her sister, Maya."

Rosamund's whole head was above the mattress now. She was listening with fierce, if skeptical, interest.

"Now, Maya." Thea chewed her lip. "Well, Maya was beautiful, too: tall, but with long black hair."

"Like that girl who came to the vet's after you."

Thea was briefly startled. She'd forgotten Rosamund had seen Blaise. "Well—uh, maybe a little. Anyway, Maya was smart and strong, too—but she didn't like having to share the leadership with Hellewise. She wanted to rule alone, and she wanted something else. To live forever."

"Sounds like a good idea to *me*," Rosamund growled.

"Well—yeah, there's nothing wrong with being immortal, I agree. Except, see, that it all depends on how much you're willing to *pay* to be it. Okay? Following me?"

"Nope."

"Well . . ." Thea floundered. Any Night Person would know immediately what she was talking about, even if by some outrageous chance they hadn't already heard the story. But of course humans were different. "Well, you see, it was a matter of what she had to do. No ordinary spell would make her immortal. She tried all sorts of things, and Hellewise even helped her. And finally they figured out what kind of spell would do it—but then Hellewise refused."

"Why?"

"Because it was too awful. No, don't *ask* me," Thea added as Rosamund's interest level immediately shot up. "I'm not going to tell you. It's not a subject for kids.'

"What, *what*? If you *don't* tell me, I'm just going to imagine even worse things."

Thea sighed. "It had to do with babies, okay? And blood. But that's not the point of this story—"

"They killed babies?"

"Not Hellewise. Maya did. And Hellewise tried to stop her, but—"

"I bet she drank the blood."

Thea stopped and looked hard at Rosamund. Human kids were ignorant, but not dumb. "Okay, yes, she drank the blood. Satisfied?"

Roz grinned, nodded, and sat back, listening avidly.

"Okay, so then Maya became immortal. But the thing was, she didn't know until afterward the price she'd have to pay. She would live forever—but only if she drank the blood of a mortal creature every day. Otherwise, she'd die."

"Like a vampire," Rosamund said with relish.

Thea was shocked for an instant, then she laughed at herself. Of course humans knew about vampires— the same way they knew about witches. Silly legends filled with misinformation.

But that meant Thea could tell her own story without fear of being believed.

"*Just* like a vampire, actually,' she said impressively, holding Rosamund's eyes. "Maya was the first vampire of all. And all her children were cursed to be vampires, too."

Roz snorted. "Vampires can't have children." She looked doubtful. "Can they?"

"The ones descended from Maya can," Thea said. She wasn't going to say the word "lamia" to a human. "It's only the kind who get made into vampires by being bitten that can't. Maya had a vampire son called Red Fern *and* she bit people. That's the story, you see—Maya wanted to make everybody like her. So she started biting people in the tribe. And eventually Hellewise decided she had to stop it."

"How?"

"Well, that was the problem. Hellewise's tribe wanted to fight with Maya and the other vampires. But Hellewise knew if they did that, they'd probably *all* get killed. Both sides. So Hellewise challenged Maya alone to a duel. Single combat."

Rosamund pushed the mattress over with a thump. "I'd fight a duel with Mr. Hendries—he's the boys' trekleader." She jumped on the mattress and attacked a pillow with hands and feet—and teeth. "I'd win, too. He's out of shape."

"Well, Hellewise didn't want to fight, but she had to. She was scared, because as a vampire Maya was a lot stronger now."

For a moment, Thea thought about it, visualizing the old story the way she had as a child. Seeing Hellewise in her white leather shift, standing in the dark forest and waiting for Maya to come. And knowing that even if she won the fight, she'd probably die—and being brave enough to *keep* standing there. Being willing to give up everything for the people she loved, and for peace.

I don't think I could ever be that brave. I mean,

I'd certainly *hope* I would be, but I have a terrible feeling that I wouldn't.

And then a strange thing happened. At that instant, she seemed to hear a voice, not her usual mind-voice, but one that was urgent and almost accusatory. Asking a question as if Thea hadn't just decided on the answer.

Would you give up everything?

Thea shifted. She didn't usually hear voices.

I suppose that's what Hellewise must have been thinking, she told herself uneasily.

"So what happened? Hey! Thea! What *happened?*" Rosamund was war-dancing on the mattress.

"Oh. Well, it was a terrible fight, but Hellewise won. She drove Maya away. And the tribe was left in peace, and they all lived happily ever after . . . um, except Hellewise. She died of her wounds."

Rosamund stopped dancing and stared in disbelief. "And you're telling me this to make me feel *better?* I never heard such a lousy story." Her chin began to tremble.

Thea forgot she was dealing with a human child. She held out her arms the way she had to Bud the puppy, the way she would have to any creature in pain—and Rosamund threw herself into them.

"No, no," Thea said, anxiously cuddling. "You see, the *point* is that Hellewise's people lived on, and they were free. And that may seem like a little thing, because they were just a little tribe, but that little tribe got bigger and bigger, and they *stayed free.* And all the witches in the world are descended from them, and they all remember Hellewise and honor her. It's a story every mother tells her daughters."

Rosamund breathed irregularly for a moment. "What about her sons?"

"Well, her sons, too. When I say 'daughters' I mean 'sons and daughters.' It's just shorter."

One green eye looked up from a mop of shaggy hair. "Like 'he' and 'him' are supposed to mean 'she' and 'her,' too?"

"Yeah." Thea thought. "I guess maybe neither is the best system." She shrugged. "The important thing is that one woman's courage kept us—them—all free."

"Look." Rosamund straightened up, staring through the hair. "Are you just jerking my chain or is that a *true* story? Because frankly you seem like a witch to me."

"That's what I was going to say," an amused voice behind Thea said.

Thea's head snapped around. The door was open a few inches and a woman was standing there. She was tall and lanky, with little glasses and long silky brown hair. Her expression reminded Thea of a look Eric got sometimes, a look of very sweet puzzlement, as if he'd suddenly been struck by one of life's overwhelming mysteries.

But that didn't matter. What mattered was that she was a stranger. An Outsider.

A human.

Thea had been blurting out the secrets of the Night World, the history of the witches, and a human adult had been listening.

Suddenly her hands and feet went numb. The golden haze disappeared, leaving her in a cold, gray reality.

"I'm sorry," the human was saying, but to Thea the voice seemed to come from a distance. "I didn't mean to startle you. I was just kidding. I really was enjoying the story—sort of a modern legend for kids, right?"

Thea's eyes focused on another human behind the adult. Eric. He'd been listening, too.

"Mom's such a kidder," he said nervously. His green eyes were apologetic—and intense. As if he were trying to make a connection with Thea.

But Thea didn't want to be connected. Couldn't be, to these people. She was surrounded by humans, trapped in one of their houses. She felt like the rattle-snake in a circle of big creatures with sticks.

Sheer, raw panic overtook her.

"You should be a writer, you know?" the human woman was saying. "All that creativity . . ." She took a step inside the room.

Thea stood up, dumping Rosamund on the floor. They were coming at her—by now, the very walls seemed to be closing in. They were alien, cruel, sadistic, terrorizing, evil, *not-her-kind*. They were Cotton Mather and the Inquisition and they *knew* about her. They were going to point at her in the street and cry "Witch!"

Thea ran.

She slipped between Eric and his mother like a frightened cat, not touching either of them. She ran down the hall, through the living room, out the door.

Outside, the sky was clouded over and it was getting dark. Thea only stopped long enough to get her bearings, then headed west, walking as fast as she could. Her heart was pounding and telling her to go faster.

Get away, get away. Go to earth. Find home.

She turned corners and zigzagged, like a fox being chased by the hounds.

She was ten minutes from the house when she heard an engine pacing her. She looked. It was Eric's jeep. Eric was driving and his mother and Rosamund were passengers.

"Thea, *stop. Please* wait." Eric stopped the jeep and jumped out.

He was on the sidewalk in front of her. Thea froze.

"Listen to me," he said in a low voice, turning away from the jeep. "I'm sorry they came, too—I couldn't stop them. Mom feels awful. She's crying, Roz is crying . . . *please*, won't you come back?"

He looked close to crying himself. Thea just felt numb.

"It's okay. I'm fine," she said at random. "I didn't mean to upset anybody." *Please let me go away*.

"Look, we shouldn't have eavesdropped. I know that. It was just . . . you're so good with Rosamund. I never saw anybody she liked so much. And . . . and . . . I *know* you're sensitive about your grandma. That's why you're upset, isn't it? That story is something she told you, isn't it?"

Dimly, somewhere in the pit of Thea's mind, a light shone. At least he thought it was a story.

"We have family stories too," Eric was saying, an edge of desperation in his voice. "My grandpa used to tell us he was a Martian—I swear to God this is true. And then he went to my kindergarten Back to School and I'd told all the kids he was a Martian, and they made these beep-beep noises at him and laughed, and I felt so bad. He was really embarrassed. . . ."

He was babbling. Thea's numbness had receded enough that she felt sorry for him. But then a shape loomed up and she tensed again. It was his mother, silky hair flying.

"Look, Thea," Eric's mother said. Her expression was wretched and earnest. "Everybody knows your grandma, knows how old she is, how she's a little . . . quirky. But if she's scaring you—if she's telling you any kind of weird stuff—"

"Mom!" Eric shouted through his teeth.

She waved a hand at him. Her little glasses were steamed up. "You don't *need* to deal with that, okay? No kid needs to deal with that. If you want a place to stay; if you need anything—if we need to call social services—"

"Mom, please, I'm *begging* you. *Shut up.*"

Social services, Thea was thinking. Dear Isis, there'll be some sort of *investigation.* The Harmans in court. Gran accused of being senile—or being part of some cult. And then the Night World coming in to enforce the law. . . .

Her terror peaked and left her deadly calm.

"It's okay," she said, turning her gaze toward Eric. Not looking at him, but going through the motions exactly. "Your mom's just trying to be helpful. But really"—she turned the same face toward his mother—"everything's okay. Gran isn't strange or anything. She does tell stories—but she doesn't scare anybody."

Is that good enough? Close enough to whatever you believe? Will it make you leave me alone?

Apparently so. "I just don't want to be responsible for you and Eric—well . . ." Eric's mom exhaled nervously, almost a laugh.

"Breaking up?" Thea made a sound that was also almost a laugh. "Don't worry. I'd never want that." She turned a smile on Eric, looking down because she couldn't meet his eyes. "I'm sorry if I got—touchy. I was just—embarrassed, I guess. Like you said about your grandpa."

"Will you come back with us? Or let us take you home?" Eric's voice was soft. He wanted her to go back to his house.

"Just home, if you don't mind. I've got homework." She lifted her eyes, making herself smile again.

Eric nodded. He didn't look happy, but he wasn't as upset as he had been.

In the backseat of the jeep, Rosamund pushed up against Thea and squeezed her hand.

"Don't be mad," she hissed, fierce as ever. "Are you mad? I'm sorry. Want me to kill somebody for you?"

"I'm not mad," Thea whispered, looking over the top of Rosamund's shaggy head. "Don't worry about it."

She had reverted to the strategy of any trapped animal. Wait and watch for your chance. Don't fight until you see a real opportunity to get away.

"See you tomorrow," Eric said as she got out of the jeep. His voice was almost a plea.

"See you tomorrow," Thea said. It wasn't time to get away yet. She waved until the jeep was gone.

Then it was time. She dashed inside, up the stairs, and straight to Blaise.

"Wait a minute," Blaise said. "Go back. So you're saying they *didn't* believe any of it."

"Right. At worst Eric's mom thinks Gran's bonkers. But it was a close call. For a while there I thought she might want to get Gran declared unfit or something."

The two of them were sitting on the floor by Blaise's bed where Thea had collapsed. Blaise was eating candy corn with one hand and scribbling on a yellow legal pad with the other, all the while listening attentively.

Because that was the thing about Blaise. She might be vain and self-centered, quarrelsome, hot-tempered, lazy, unkind to humans, and generally hard to live with, but she came through for family. She was a witch.

I'm sorry I said you might be a little like Maya, Thea thought.

"It's my fault," she said out loud.

"Yes, it is," Blaise said, scribbling.

"I should have just found some way to keep him at a distance in the beginning."

But of course, it was because of Blaise that she hadn't. She'd thought Eric was safer with her than he would have been with Blaise. She'd thought that somehow . . . somehow . . .

Things would work out. That was it. There had always been some secret underlying hope that there could be a future with Eric. Some little hiding place where she'd kept the hope that things could be all right.

But now she had to face reality.

There was no future.

The only thing she could give Eric was death. And that was all he could give her. She'd realized that, all in one terrible explosion of insight when she'd seen Eric's mother in the room.

There was no way for them to be together without being discovered. Even if they ran away, someday, somewhere, the Night People would find them. They'd be brought before the joint Night World Council, the vampire and witch elders. And then the law would be fulfilled. . . .

Thea had never seen an execution, but she'd heard of them. And if the Harmans tried to stop the Council from killing her, it would start a war. Witches against vampires. Maybe even witches against witches. It could mean the end of everything.

"So it doesn't look like we have to kill the mother," Blaise said, frowning at her scribbles. "On the other hand, if we kill the kids, the mother's bound to be unhappy, and might make a connection. So to be safe—"

"We can't kill any of them," Thea said. Her voice was muted but final.

"I don't mean *ourselves*. I'm going to call one of our friendly vampire cousins. Ash—he's supposed to be out on the West Coast somewhere, isn't he? Or

Quinn, he likes that kind of thing. One quick bite, let the blood run out—"

"Blaise, I am not going to let vampires kill Eric. Or anybody," she added as Blaise opened her mouth. "It's not *necessary*. Nobody needs to die."

"So you have a better idea?"

Thea looked at a statue of Isis, the Queen of Egyptian Goddesses, on the desk. "I . . . don't know. I thought of the Cup of Lethe. Make them forget everything about me. But it might look suspicious—this entire family with a gap in their memory. And kids at school would wonder why Eric doesn't remember my name anymore."

"True."

Thea stared at the moon held between Isis's golden horns. Her brain, which had been working so coldly and logically, helping her to survive, was stalling now. There had to be a way to save Eric and his family—or what was the point of living herself?

Then she saw it.

"What I really think would be best," she said slowly, because it hurt like a physical pain, "would be for Eric to stop caring about me. To fall in love with someone else."

Blaise sat back. She stirred the candy corn with long, elegant nails. She ate a piece.

"I admire you," she said. "Very sensible."

"*Not* you," Thea said through clenched teeth. "You understand that, right? A human. If he falls in love with another girl he'll forget about me without any Lethe. Nobody will disappear or have amnesia; nobody will get suspicious."

"Okay. Although I would've liked to try him. He's got a strong will—I think he'd have held out for a while. Been a challenge."

Thea ignored this. "I still have some of his blood. The question is, do you have something you've been holding back, some love spell that will completely blow him out of the water?"

Blaise ate another piece of candy corn. "Of course I do." She narrowed her gray eyes. "Also, of course, it's a forbidden spell."

"I figured. Blaise, I'm now the princess of forbidden spells. One more doesn't matter. But I'll do the actual working, I don't want you to get in trouble."

"You won't like it. It involves the bezoar stone from the stomach of an ibex—which I just happened to pick up while we were living with Aunt Gerdeth."

Ibex were an endangered species. But this one was already dead. "I'll do the working," Thea said stubbornly.

"You really care about him, don't you?"

"Yes," Thea whispered. "I still think we're soul-mates. But . . ."

Would you give up everything?

"I don't want to be the reason he dies. Or the reason a war starts between the Harmans and the rest of the Night World. And if I have to give him up, I'd rather do it myself, make sure he's safe with somebody else who loves him."

"Have you got somebody picked out?"

"Her name is Pilar." Thea looked at her cousin suddenly. "Blaise? When Luke asked you what you

wanted, and you said nothing you could have . . .
what did you mean?''

Blaise tilted her head back and examined the ceiling. Then she looked down. "Does anybody ever
want anything they can have? Really?"

"I . . . don't know."

Blaise clasped her knees and rested her chin on
them. "If we can have things, we don't really want
them anymore. So there's always something out
there that we're wanting and not able to get . . . and
maybe that's *good.*''

It didn't sound good to Thea. It sounded like one
of those terrible lessons in Life 101 that were supposed to make you more mature.

"Let's do the spell," she said.

CHAPTER

13

You know, he probably only loved you because of
the yemonja," Blaise said.

Thea looked up from her seat in the empty chemis-
try lab. It was morning break, and this was the most
private place they could find at school. "Thanks,
Blaise. I needed that."

But maybe it was true. She'd almost forgotten that
she'd used a spell to get him in the first place.

That should make a difference, she told herself. If
it was all artificial, I shouldn't even miss it.

She still felt as if she were encased in ice.

"Did you get it?"

"Sure." Blaise tossed a ring on the high table. "I
asked her if I could look at it, then pretended I
dropped it in the bushes. She's still out there
searching."

Thea pulled the binding spell out of her backpack.

Two anatomically correct dolls, both made with the blue wax Blaise used for her jewelry. Beautiful little creatures—Blaise was an artist. The male one contained the Kleenex with Eric's blood and a single sandy hair Thea had found clinging to her shoulder.

Thea put Pilar's turquoise ring around the feet of the female doll and tied it with a red thread to keep it on. She held out a hand.

From her backpack, Blaise produced a corked hexagonal bottle. The liquid inside was made up of all sorts of disgusting things, including ground bezoar stone. Thea held her breath as she poured it over the two figures, which immediately began to smoke.

"Now bind them together," Blaise said, coughing and waving a hand to clear a space to breathe.

"I know." Thea took a thin scarlet ribbon seven feet long and patiently began winding it around the two figures. It wrapped them like mummies. She tucked the loose end into a loop.

"And there they are," Blaise said. "Bound till death. Congratulations. Let's see, it's ten fifteen now, so he should have forgotten your existence by about . . . say, ten sixteen." She reached up and her hair ran like black water through her hands as she stretched.

Thea tried to smile.

The pain was bad. It was as if some part of Thea's physical body had been cut off. She felt raw and bleeding and not at all able to deal with things like French or trigonometry.

There must be more to life. I'll go somewhere and

do something for other people; I'll work in third world countries or try to save an endangered species.

But thinking about future good works didn't help the raw ache. Or the feeling that if the ache stopped she would just be numb and never be happy again.

And all this for a human . . .

It didn't work anymore. She couldn't go back to her old way of thinking. Humans might be alien, but they were still people. They were as good as witches. Just different.

She managed to get through the schoolday without running into Eric—which mainly meant scuttling around corridors after bells rang and being tardy for classes. She was scuttling after the last bell toward Dani's U.S. government class when she almost collided with Pilar.

"Thea!"

The voice was surprised. Thea looked up.

Deep amber-brown eyes, framed by spiky black lashes. Pilar was looking at her very strangely.

Wondering at your good luck? Thea thought. Has Eric proposed to you yet? "What?" she said.

Pilar hesitated, then just shook her head and walked off.

Thea ducked into the history classroom.

Dani said, "Thea!"

Everybody sounds the same.

"Where've you *been*? Eric's looking all over for you."

Of course, I should have realized. Blaise was wrong—he's not just going to forget about me and walk away. He's a gentleman; he's going to *tell* me he's walking away.

"Can I go home with you?" she asked Dani wretchedly. "I need some space."

"Thea . . ." Dani dragged her to a corner and looked her over with anxious eyes. "Eric really wants to find you . . . but what's wrong?" she whispered. "Is it something about Suzanne? The old gym's still closed, isn't it?"

"It's nothing to do with that." She was about to suggest they get moving when a tall figure walked in the door.

Eric.

He walked straight to Thea.

The kids hanging around the teacher's desk were looking. The teacher was looking. Thea felt like a freak show.

"We have to talk," Eric said flatly.

She'd never seen him look quite like this before. He was pale, glassy-eyed, hollow-cheeked. He somehow managed to look as if he'd missed a week's worth of sleep since that morning.

And he was right. They had to talk to end it. She had to explain that it was okay, or he'd never be able to go.

I can do that.

"Somewhere private," Thea said.

They left Dani and walked through the campus, past the old gym with its yellow ribbon of police tape hanging limp and still. Through the football field. Thea didn't know where they were going, and suspected Eric didn't either—they just kept moving until they were out of sight of *people*.

The green of the tended grass gave way to yellow-green, and then brown, and then desert. Thea wrapped her arms around herself, thinking about how cold it had gotten in just a week and a half. The last trace of summer was gone.

And now we're going to talk about it, she thought as Eric stopped. Okay. I don't have to *think*, just say the right words. She forced herself to look at him.

He turned the haggard, haunted face on her and said, "I want you to stop it."

Funny choice of words. You mean end it, break it off, put it quietly out of its misery.

She couldn't get all that out, so she just said, "What?"

"I don't know what you're doing," he said, "but I want it stopped. Now."

His green eyes were level. Not apologetic, more like demanding. His voice was flat.

Thea had a sudden sense of shifting realities. All the hairs on her arms were standing up.

Caught without a working brain, she said, "I—what are you talking about?"

"You know what I'm talking about." He was still looking at her steadily.

Thea shook her head no.

He shrugged. It was a you-asked-for-it shrug. "Whatever you're doing," he said with terrible distinctness, "to try and make me like Pilar, it has got to stop. Because it's not fair to her. She's upset right now because I'm acting crazy. But I don't want to be with her. It's you I love. And if you want to get rid of me, then *tell* me, but don't try and foist me off on somebody else."

Thea listened to the whole speech feeling as if she were floating several feet above the ground. The sky and desert seemed too bright, not warm, just very shiny. While her brain ran around frantically like Madame Curie in a new cage, she managed to get out, "What could I possibly have to do—with you liking Pilar?"

Eric looked around, found a rock, and sat on it. He stared down at his hands for a minute or so. Finally he looked up, his expression helpless.

"Give me a break, Thea," he said. "How stupid do you think I am?"

Oh.

"Oh." Then she thought, don't just *stand* there. You bluffed him before. You talked him out of knowing he'd been bitten by a snake. For *Earth's* sake, you can talk him out of whatever he's thinking now.

"Eric—I guess we've all been under a lot of stress. . . ."

"Oh, please don't give me that." He seemed to be talking to a clump of silver cholla, eyeing the halos of awful spines as if he might jump into them. *"Please* don't give me that."

He took a deep breath and spoke deliberately. "You charm snakes and read guinea pigs' minds. You cure rattler bites with a touch. You tap into people's brains. You make up magical potpourri bags and your insane cousin is the goddess Aphrodite." He looked at her. "Did I miss anything?"

Thea found another rock and backed up to it blindly. She sat. Of everything in the universe, right then what she was most aware of was her own breathing.

"I have this feeling," Eric said, watching her with his green eyes, "that you guys are in fact the descendants of good old Hecate Witch-Queen. Am I close?"

"You think you win a prize?" Thea still couldn't think, couldn't put a meaningful remark together. Could only gabble.

He paused and grinned, a wry and painful grin, but the first one she'd seen today. Then the smile faded. "It's true, isn't it?" he said simply.

Thea looked out over the desert, toward the huge, bare cliffs of rock in the distance. She let her eyes unfocus, soaking in the expanse of brown-green. Then she put her fingers to the bridge of her nose.

She was going to do something that all her ancestors would condemn her for, something that nobody she'd grown up with would understand.

"It's true," she whispered.

He breathed out, a lonely human figure in that vastness of the desert.

"How long have you known?" she asked.

"I . . . don't know. I mean, I think I always sort of knew. But it wasn't possible—and you didn't want me to know. So I *didn't* know." A kind of excitement was creeping into his haggardness. "It's really true, then. You can do magic."

Say it, Thea told herself. You've done everything else. Say the words to a human.

"I'm a witch."

"A Hearth-Woman, I thought you called it. That's what Roz was telling me."

At that, Thea was horrified out of her daze of horror. Stricken. "Eric—you can't talk about this with *Roz*. You don't *understand*. They'll *kill* her."

He didn't look as shocked as she might have expected. "I knew you were scared of something. I thought it was just that people might hurt *you*—and your grandma."

"They will; they'll kill me. But they'll kill you and Roz, too—and your mom and any other human they think may have learned about them—"

"*Who* will?"

She looked at him, floundered a moment, and then made the ultimate betrayal of her upbringing.

"It's called the Night World."

"Okay," he said slowly, half an hour later. They were sitting side by side on his rock. Thea wasn't touching him, although her whole side was aware of his presence.

"Okay, so basically, the descendants of Maya are lamia and the descendants of Hellewise are witches. And together they're all this big secret organization, the Night World."

"Yes." Thea had to fight the instinct to whisper. "It's not just lamia and witches, though. It's shapeshifters and made vampires and werewolves and other things. All the races that the human race couldn't deal with."

"Vampires," Eric muttered to the cholla, his eyes going glassy again. "That's what really gets me, real

vampires. I don't know why, it follows logically. . . ."
He looked at Thea, his gaze sharpening. "Look, if all
you people have supernatural powers, why don't you
just take over?"

"Not enough of us," Thea said. "And too many of
you. It doesn't matter how supernatural we are."

"But, look—"

"You breed much faster, have more children—and
you *kill* us whenever you find us. The witches were
on the verge of extinction before they got together
with the other races and formed the Night World.
And that's why Night World law is so strict about
keeping our secrets from humans."

"And that's why you tried to hand me over to
Pilar," Eric said.

Thea could feel his eyes on her like a physical sen-
sation. She stared at a patch of rock nettle between
her feet. "I didn't want you dead. I didn't want me
dead, either."

"And they'd really kill us for being in love."

"In a *minute*."

He touched her shoulder. Thea could feel warmth
spread from his hand and she had to work to make
sure she didn't tremble. "Then we'll keep it a secret,"
he said.

"Eric, it's not like that. You don't understand.
There's nowhere we could go, no place we could
hide. The Night People are everywhere."

"And they all follow these same rules."

"*Yes*. It's what allows them to survive."

He breathed for a moment, then said in a voice
that had gone husky, "There's got to be a way."

"That's what I let myself think—for a while." Her own voice sounded shaky. "But we have to face reality. The only *chance* we have of even living through this is for us to just go our separate ways. And for you to try as hard as you can to forget me and everything I've told you."

She *was* trembling now, and her eyes had filled. But her hands were balled into fists and she wouldn't look at him.

"Thea—"

The tears spilled. *"I won't be your death!"*

"And I can't forget you! I can't stop loving you."

"Well, and maybe that was just a spell, too," she said, sniffling. Tears were falling straight off her face and onto the rock. Eric looked around for something to give her, then tried to wipe her wet cheeks with his thumb.

She whacked his hand away. *"Listen* to me. You did miss something when you were adding up what I did. I also make love spells for *me.* I put one on you, and that's why you fell in love in the first place."

Eric didn't look impressed. "When?"

"When did I put the spell on you? The day I asked you to the dance."

Eric laughed.

"You—"

"Thea." He shook his head. "Look," he said gently, "I fell in love with you *before* that. It was when we were out here with that snake. When we just looked at each other and . . . and . . . I saw you surrounded by mist and you were the most beautiful thing in the world." He shook his head again. "And maybe *that* was magic, but I don't think it was any spell you were putting on me."

Thea wiped her eyes on her sleeve. Okay, so the yemonja had nothing to do with it. Anyway, love spells just seemed to bounce off Eric—even the dolls hadn't worked. . . .

She bent suddenly and picked up her backpack. "And I don't know *why* this didn't work," she muttered. She took out a quilted makeup bag, unzipped it, and reached inside.

The dolls came out as a bundle. At first glance they looked all right. Then Thea saw it.

The male doll had turned around. Instead of being face-to-face with the female doll, it had its back to her.

The scarlet ribbon was still wound tightly around them. There was no way that it could have slipped, that this could have happened by accident. But the dolls had been inside the case, and the case had been inside her backpack all day.

Eric was watching. "That's Pilar's ring. Hey, is that the spell on me and Pilar? Can I see it?"

"Oh, why not?" Thea whispered. She felt dazed again.

So it couldn't have been an accident, and no human could have done it. And no witch could have done it either.

Maybe . . .

Maybe there was a magic stronger than spells. Maybe the soulmate principle was responsible, and if two people were meant to be together, nothing could keep them apart.

Eric was gingerly unwinding the scarlet ribbon. "I'll give the ring back to Pilar," he said. He reduced the binding spell to its constituent parts, put them gently back in the makeup bag.

Then he looked at her.

"I've always loved you," he said. "The only question is . . ." He broke off and looked like the shy Eric she knew again. "Is, do you love me?" he finished at last. His voice was soft, but he was looking at her steadily.

Maybe there are some things you just can't fight. . . .

She made herself look at him. The image wobbled and split.

"I love you," she whispered. "I don't know what's going to happen, but I do."

They fell—slow as a dream, but still falling—into each other's arms.

"There's a problem," Thea said some time later. "Besides all the other problems. I'm going to be doing something next week, and I just need you to give me some time."

"What kind of something?"

"I can't tell you."

"You have to tell me," he said calmly, his breath against her hair. "You have to tell me everything now."

"It's magic stuff and it's dangerous—" A second too late she realized her mistake.

"What do you mean, dangerous?" He straightened up. His voice told her the peaceful interlude was over. "If you think I'm going to let you do something dangerous by yourself . . ."

He wore her down. He was good at that—even better than his sister—and Thea was no good at refusing him. In the end she told him about Suzanne Blanchet.

"A dead witch," he said.

"A spirit. And a very angry one."

"And you think she's coming back," he said.

"I think she's been here all along. Maybe hanging around the old gym, which hasn't done her any good since nobody's been there assaulting dummies. But if they open it to have the Halloween party . . ."

"It'll be full of humans, all visiting those booths, all reminding her of what she hates. She can pick them off like ticks off a dog."

"Something like that. I think it could be bad. So what I've got to do is quietly lure her somewhere else and then send her back where she came from."

"And how are you going to do that?"

"I don't know." Thea rubbed her forehead. The sun was dipping toward the cliffs and long afternoon shadows had fallen across the desert.

"You've got a plan," Eric said matter-of-factly.

Not you, Thea thought. I promised myself I wouldn't use you. Not even to save lives.

"You've got a plan you think is dangerous for humans. For me, since I'm going to be helping you."

I will not use you. . . .

"Let's make this easy on everybody. You *know* I'm not going to let you do it alone. We might as well take that as given and go on from there."

This is the crazy guy who ignores snakebites and attacks people with punch, she reminded herself. Do you *really* expect to talk him out of helping you?

But if something were to happen to him . . .

The voice came back again, and Thea didn't understand it and she didn't like it at all.

Would you give up everything?

CHAPTER

14

A week passed more or less quietly. Grandma Harman came home, her cough better. She didn't seem to notice anything different about Thea.

Night came earlier, and everyone at school talked about parties and costumes. The air got colder and there was an announcement that the old gym would be opened for Halloween.

Thea heard that Randy Marik had been moved to a psychiatric hospital and was in intensive therapy. He was making some progress.

Thea and Eric worked every day on their plan.

The only real excitement came the night when Thea walked in, sat on Blaise's bed, and said, "Bullets won't stop him."

"*What?*" Blaise looked up from creaming her elbows.

"I mean, spells won't stop him. Eric. They just

177

bounce off. I'm telling you this because you're going to notice that he's not with Pilar."

Blaise snapped the tube of cream shut. She stared at Thea for a full minute before she said tightly, "What are you saying?"

Thea's humor drained away. She looked at the floor. "I'm saying we're soulmates," she said quietly. "And that I can't help it. There is really, truly, nothing I can do about it."

"I can't believe, after all that—"

"Right. After all that work. And after me trying and trying to stop, because I'm scared to death. But there's no way to *fight* it, Blaise. That's what I'm trying to tell you. I've got to find some way to try to live with it." She looked at her cousin. "Okay?"

"You know it's not okay. You know it's completely not okay."

"I guess what I mean is, okay, will you please not kill him or turn us in? Because I can't stand being in another fight with you. And I can't stop breaking the law."

Blaise tossed the cream jar in the direction of the dresser. "Thea, are you all right?" she said, seriously. "Because you're acting very . . ."

"Fatalistic?"

"Fatalistic and generally scary."

"I'm okay. I just . . . I don't know what's going to happen, but I am sort of . . . calm. I'm going to do my best. Eric's going to do his best. And beyond that, nothing's guaranteed."

Blaise stared for another minute, her gray eyes searching Thea's face. Then she shook her head. "I won't turn you in. You *know* I would never turn you in. We're sisters. And as for trying to kill him . . ." She shrugged, looking grim. "It probably wouldn't work. That guy is impossible."

"Thank you, Blaise." Thea touched her cousin's arm lightly.

Blaise covered Thea's hand with her own red-nailed fingers, just for a moment. Then she sat back and straightened her pillows with a little jerk.

"Just don't *tell* me anything, all right? I wash my hands of you two and I don't want to know what's going on. Besides, I've got worries of my own. I have to decide between a Maserati and a Karmann Ghia."

Halloween.

Thea looked out the window at the darkened world. There weren't any kids in the alley, but she knew they were flitting around the city. Goblins and ghosts and witches and vampires—all fakes. Real vampires were sitting inside at fireplaces, or maybe at exclusive parties, chuckling.

And real witches were getting dressed for their Samhain Circles.

Thea put on a white shift, sleeveless, made out of one piece of material. She pulled a soft white belt around her waist and made a loop pointing up with one side of the tie, then wrapped the other end around the base of the loop three times. A thet knot. Witches had used them for four thousand years.

She took a breath and looked outside again.

Enjoy the peace while you can, she told herself. It's going to be a busy night.

Eric's jeep pulled into the alley. The horn honked once.

Thea grabbed the backpack, which had been stuffed under her bed. It was full of materials. Oak, ash, quassia chips, blessed thistle, mandrake root. The hardened residue from the bronze bowl, which she had painstakingly scraped off with one of Blaise's art knives. A wooden seal, also carved with Blaise's tools. And an ounce vial with three precious drops of summoning potion stolen from the malachite bottle.

She started for the stairs.

"Hey, are you leaving already?" Blaise said, emerging from the bathroom. "You've got—what?—an hour and a half before Circle."

Blaise looked gorgeous, and more herself than at any other time of year. Her shift was black, also sleeveless, also made in one piece. Her hair hung loose to her hips, woven with little bells. Her arms were pale and beautiful against the darkness of hair and shift, and she was barefoot, wearing one ankle bracelet.

"I'm going to run out and do something before Circle," Thea said. "Don't ask me what."

Blaise of course didn't know what Thea and Eric were planning. Not even Dani knew. It was better that way.

"Thea . . ." Blaise stood at the top of the stairs and looked down as Thea dashed out. "You be *careful!*"

Thea waved at her cousin.

The back of the jeep was full of wood.

"I thought I'd better bring some more, just in case we need it," Eric said, throwing her backpack in.

Then he added in a different voice, "You look—amazing—like that."

She smiled at him. "Thanks. It's traditional. You look nice, too."

He was wearing the costume of a seventeenth-century French soldier at Ronchain—or as close as they could get from looking at woodcuts in old books.

They drove into the desert, past the huge bare cliffs, off the main road and far out among the Joshua trees, until they found the place. It was tiny, just a dip in the ground almost enclosed in red sandstone pillars. The pillars didn't look like the monoliths at Stonehenge—they were knobby and squished sideways, like towers of Play-doh that some kid had smashed—but they served the same purpose.

They'd found this place all by themselves, and Thea was very proud of it.

"The fire's still going," she said. "That's good."

It had been burning for the last three days inside the circle. Thea's hope had been that it would keep Suzanne interested—and away from the people setting up in the old gym. And it seemed to have worked.

Not just the fire, of course. The three dummies lying on the ground tied to stakes were supposed to be interesting, too.

"These guys all look okay," Eric said. He picked up the smallest dummy and dusted it off. It looked something like a scarecrow when he thrust the stick into a hole in the ground, standing it up.

A scarecrow dressed in a black shift tied with a thet knot. With a sign hanging around the neck: LUCIENNE.

The other small dummy had a sign that said CLÉM-ENT. The big dummy's sign said SUZANNE.

"Okay," Thea said when they had unloaded the wood, leaving her backpack in the jeep. "Now, remember, you don't do *anything* until I get back, right? Not anything. And if I'm a few minutes late, you just wait."

He stopped nodding. "The Halloween party starts at nine. If you're not here at nine exactly, I might—"

"*No.* Don't touch anything, don't do anything."

"Thea, we might lose her. What if she decides that nothing's happening here, so she might as well go to the party—"

"I won't be late," Thea said flatly. It seemed the only way to win the argument. "But do *not* burn those witches before I'm here to cast the circle. Okay?"

"Good luck," he said.

He looked handsome and mysterious in his exotic clothes. Not like himself. They kissed under the half-full moon.

"Be safe," Thea whispered, making herself let go of him.

"Come back safe," he whispered. "I love you."

She drove the jeep back to the city, to the maidens' Circle Twilight meeting.

It was being held this year at a Night World club on the southern edge of town. There was no sign on the door, but the doormat, between two grinning jack-o'-lanterns, had been painted with a black dahlia.

Thea knocked and the door opened.

"Dani! You look great."

"So do you," Dani said. She was dressed in white,

in a pleated sheer gown that hung to her ankles and looked Egyptian. Black braids clasped with silver cascaded from a sort of crown at her head, falling over her shoulders and back and arms. She made a beautiful Queen Isis. "You didn't wear a costume," she said, making it a question.

"Blaise and I are sort of going as Maya and Hellewise," Thea said. The truth was that she was most comfortable in her ordinary Circle clothes, and that Blaise knew she looked best in *hers*.

"Well, come on down. You're the last one," Dani said, taking Thea's hand.

They went down a flight of stairs to an underground room. It had a makeshift, thrown-together look, with crates to sit on, and white fairy lights strung between concrete pillars. Metal chairs had been pushed to the periphery.

"Thea! Hey, there! Merry meet!" people called. Thea turned around and around, smiling and getting hugs.

"Good Samhain," she kept saying. "Unity."

For those few minutes, she forgot about what was going to happen tonight. It was so good to see them all again, all her friends from summer Circles.

Kishi Hirata, dressed as Amaterasu, the Japanese sun goddess, in gold and orange. Alaric Breedlove—the sophomore from Lake Mead High—as Tammuz the shepherd, son of the mother goddess Ishtar. Claire Blessingway as the Navajo goddess Changing Woman, in a dress decorated with red flower petals and turquoise. Nathaniel Long as Herne, Celtic god of the hunt, in forest green, with stag's antlers.

Humans put on costumes to disguise themselves

tonight. Witches put on costumes to try to reflect their inner selves—what they were inside, what they wanted to be.

"Here, taste," Claire said, handing Thea a paper cup. It was full of a thick red herb drink spiced with cinnamon and cloves. "It's hibiscus—my dad's recipe."

Someone else was passing around shortbread cakes in the shape of crescent moons. Thea took one. Everything here was so bright, so warm—and she would have been so happy if all she had to do tonight was enjoy it. Have a normal Samhain Circle. Celebrate . . .

But Eric was waiting out there in the dark and cold of the desert. And Thea was counting the minutes until she could leave.

"Okay, people, it's time to get started."

Lawai'a Ikua, a pretty, sturdy girl with hair like black nylon, was standing in the center of the room. She was wearing a red shift and lei—Pele, the Hawaiian fire goddess, Thea guessed.

"Let's get our circle, here. That's good, come on. Chang Xi, you're the youngest now."

A little girl with big almond-shaped eyes came shyly into the ring of people. Thea hadn't seen her before—she must have turned seven since the last summer Circle. She was dressed in jade green as Kuan Yin, the Chinese goddess of compassion.

Still shy, she took a sprig of broom—real broom, the plant—and swept the area inside the ring.

"Thea, you do the salt."

Thea was surprised and pleased. She took the bowl of sea salt that Lawai'a offered, and walked slowly around the perimeter of the circle, sprinkling it.

"Alaric, you take the water—"

Lawai'a broke off, looking toward the stairway, seeming startled. Thea saw other people look. She turned around.

Two adults, mothers, were coming down the stairs. As the light shone on the first woman's face, Thea felt a jolt.

It was Aunt Ursula.

In a gray suit, her expression as bleak as Thea had ever seen it.

Nobody in the room made a noise. They all stood still as Joshua trees, watching until the women reached the bottom. Interrupting a Circle in the middle of casting was unheard of.

"Good Samhain," Lawai'a said faintly.

"Good Samhain." Aunt Ursula was polite, but she didn't smile. Like a displeased teacher. "I'm very sorry to bother you, but this will only take a minute."

Thea's heart had begun to pound, slow and hard.

It's just guilty conscience, she tried to tell herself. This doesn't *have* to be about you.

But it did. And something inside her knew even before Aunt Ursula looked the Circle over and said, "Thea Sophia Harman."

As if she doesn't know what I look like, Thea thought dazedly.

She clamped down hard on a wild impulse simply to brush past Aunt Ursula and head for the street. Now she knew why rabbits were so stupid as to leave a good hiding place and run blindly when a dog came near. Just panic, that's all.

She stepped away from a staring Kishi on her left

and a dismayed Nat on her right. She could feel every pair of eyes in the place on her.

"What is it?" she said, trying to look surprised.

Aunt Ursula's eyes met hers directly, as if to say, *You know*. But she didn't say anything, which was almost as bad.

"Dani Naete Mella Abforth."

Oh, *Eileithyia*. Not Dani, too. . . .

Dani was stepping out of the circle. Her small head was held proudly, but Thea could see the fear in her eyes. She walked, linen swaying around her ankles, to stand beside Thea.

Dani, I'm sorry. . . .

"That's all," Aunt Ursula said. "The rest of you go on with your Circle. Good Samhain, everybody." To Thea and Dani, she said, "You need to come outside."

They followed her silently. There was nothing else to do.

When they were out in the cool night air, Dani said, "Is—something wrong?" She looked from Aunt Ursula to the other woman, who was short but had considerable presence.

And seemed familiar to Thea . . . and then she had it.

It's Nana Buruku. From the Inner Circle.

This isn't a Harman family matter. The Inner Circle itself is calling us.

"There are some things we need to talk about. Come on and let's get it all cleared up fast," Nana Buruku said quietly, putting a cinnamon-colored hand on Thea's arm. Gran's ancient Lincoln Continental was sitting at the curb. Nana Buruku took the wheel herself.

Dani and Thea held hands in the backseat. Dani's fingers were icy cold.

The car wound up and down streets lined with human trick-or-treaters, to a big ranch-style house with high block walls screening the backyard. Selene's house, Thea realized, seeing the name Lucna on the mailbox.

It must be where they're having the maidens' Circle Midnight meeting.

Aunt Ursula got out. Thea and Dani sat in the car with Nana Buruku. In a few minutes, Aunt Ursula came back with Blaise.

Selene, dressed in silver, and Vivienne in black, followed as far as the driveway. They looked sober and scared, not like wicked witches at all.

Blaise did. Barefoot and apparently indifferent to the cold, little bells ringing, she looked flushed and angry and proud. She opened the door with a jerk and sat down hard beside Thea, who scooted over.

"What's going on?" she said, almost out loud. "I'm missing the moon cakes, I'm missing *everything*. What kind of Samhain is this?"

Thea had never admired her more.

"We'll get back in time," Dani said, and her voice was steady, even if her fingers were still cold.

They're both brave, Thea thought. And me? But however much she wanted to, she couldn't get a word out through the tightness in her throat.

She half expected Nana Buruku to get on the freeway and head out toward the desert, toward Thierry's land. But instead the Lincoln headed down familiar streets and pulled up in the alley behind Grandma Harman's store.

Thea could feel Dani's questioning eyes on her. But she had no idea what was going on, and she was afraid to look Dani in the face.

"Come on," Aunt Ursula said, and shepherded them through the back door, into the shop, through the bead curtain that led to the workshop.

All the chairs for Gran's students had been pushed into a rough circle. People were sitting in them, or standing and talking quietly, but when Thea stepped through the curtain behind Nana Buruku, they all stopped and looked.

Thea's eyes moved from face to face, seeing each in a sort of disconnected, dreamlike flash. Grandma Harman, looking so grim and tired. Mother Cybele, who was *the* Mother of the Inner Circle, just as Gran was *the* Crone, looking anxious. Aradia, the Maiden, her lovely face serious and sad.

Others she recognized from two years ago, people who were so famous she knew them by their first names. Rhys, Belfana, Creon, Old Bob.

Aunt Ursula and Nana Buruku made up the last two of the nine.

They looked like ordinary people, working men and women and still-sharp-as-a-tack retired seniors, the kind you'd see any day on the street.

They weren't.

This was the biggest concentration of magical talent anywhere in the world. These people were the witch geniuses, the prodigies and the sages, the far-seers, the teachers, the policy-makers. They were the Inner Circle.

And they were all looking at Thea.

"The girls are here," Mother Cybele said softly to Aradia. "They're standing in the middle."

Gran said, "All right, let's get this thing started. Will everybody find themselves a seat." It wasn't a question, it was an order. Gran was senior to all these celebrities.

But she wouldn't *look* at Thea. And that was the most terrible, nightmarish thing of all. She acted as if Thea and Blaise were strangers.

Everyone was sitting, nudging their chairs into a more evenly spaced circle. They were all wearing their ordinary clothes, Thea realized: business suits or uniforms or pants and tops. In Aradia's case, jeans. In Old Bob's case, dirty overalls.

Which means they never even started their own ceremony tonight. This is important enough to skip Samhain over.

This is a trial.

Red-haired Belfana pushed Creon's wheelchair to an empty spot. She was the last to sit down.

I'm centered, Thea thought numbly.

It was her worst fear, the very thing that had driven her away from Eric in the desert, the first time she'd felt the soulmate connection with him. And now it was *true*.

She could hear Dani breathing irregularly, and the faint tinkle of bells as Blaise shifted from foot to foot.

"All right," Grandma Harman said, sounding tired but formal. "By Earth, by Air, by Water, and by Fire,

I call this Circle to unity." She went on, reciting the age-old formula for a meeting of deliberation.

For Thea, the words blended into the pounding of blood in her ears. It was strange, how terrifying it could be to be surrounded in all directions by people. Everywhere she looked, another grave, unreadable face. She felt as trapped as if they had been humans.

"Thea Sophia Harman," Gran said, and suddenly Thea was listening again. "You stand accused . . ."

There seemed to be an endless, empty pause, although Thea knew it was probably no time at all.

". . . of working forbidden spells in direct disobedience to the laws of Hellewise and of this Circle. . . ."

All Thea heard for a while was *"working forbidden spells."* It seemed to hang in the air, echoing. Part of her kept waiting to hear the other, more terrible charges of betraying the secrets of the Night World and falling in love with a human. But they didn't come.

". . . summoning a spirit from the far places beyond the veil . . . binding two humans with a forbidden love charm . . ."

And then Gran was reading Blaise's name.

Blaise was charged with fashioning a necklace out of forbidden materials and binding humans with a forbidden charm. Dani was charged with aiding and abetting Thea in the summoning of a spirit from the far places—which was wrong, of course, Thea thought dizzily.

Her whole body was tingling, from the soles of her feet, to her palms, to her scalp. With fear . . . and with something like relief.

They don't know. They don't know the worst part of it, or they would have said so—wouldn't they? And if I just keep quiet, why should they ever know?

Then she focused on Gran, who had finished reading the charges and was now talking in an ordinary voice again. "And I have to say that I'm disappointed in all three of you. Especially you, Thea. I'd expect this from *her*, of course"—she nodded at Blaise, speaking to the rest of the Circle—"that descendant of mine there who's dressed up like Hecate's bad daughter. But I honestly thought Thea had more sense."

She *looked* disappointed. And that—hurt. Thea had always been the good girl, the golden girl, youngest and most promising of the Hearth-Woman line. Now, as she looked from face to face, she saw disappointment everywhere.

I've failed them; I've disgraced my heritage. I'm so ashamed. . . .

She wanted to curl up and disappear.

Just then, there was a silvery ripple of bells. Blaise was tossing her dark head. She looked defiant and scornful and very proud and a little bored.

"What *I* want to know is who turned us in," she said in an almost inaudible but definitely menacing whisper. "Whoever it is, they're going to be *sorry*."

And suddenly, somehow, Thea was less frightened. The disappointment didn't mean so much. It was possible to shock the Inner Circle and still be standing up. Blaise proved it.

It was then that irony struck Thea. She'd spent her life getting in trouble because of Blaise, and now here they were, in the worst trouble imaginable—because of her.

And Dani was in trouble, too. Her velvety eyes were filled with tears. When she saw *that*, Thea found the tightness in her throat easing. She could talk again.

"Look—excuse me—but there's something you need to know. Before this goes any further—"

"You'll have a chance to speak later," Mother Cybele said, her voice soft and firm, like her little dumpling-shaped body.

"No, I have to say it now." Thea turned to Gran, speaking, for just these few seconds, to her grandmother rather than to the Crone of the Inner Circle. "Grandma, Dani shouldn't be here. Really. *Really*. She didn't know anything about the summoning; I did it all. I *promise*."

Gran's expression gentled slightly, the creases on her face shifting. Then she was impassive again.

"All right, all right, we'll see about that later. The first thing is to find out just what *you've* been doing. Since you seem to be the instigator here."

It was when she said "later" that realization hit Thea like a tsunami. And everything changed.

Later . . . time . . . *what time is it?*

She looked frantically around for the clock. There—behind Old Bob's gray head . . .

Ten minutes to ten.

Eric.

Somehow, in the stress she'd felt since Aunt Ursula came to get her, she had completely forgotten that he was waiting in the desert.

But now she could *see* him, the vision in her mind's eye as clear as if she were standing there with him. Eric watching the clock, minutes going by, and Thea still not arriving. Eric looking at the bonfire and at the three black-clothed dummies tied to their stakes.

And the party. The Halloween party at school. Blistered metal doors being opened and people flooding in. Shoes walking across the scuffed wooden floor, costumed kids standing underneath the dangling witch figures. Kids shrieking with laughter, handing over goblin money, crowding into the torture booths.

While something lurked around the exposed pipes on the ceiling. Maybe invisible, maybe looking like a white figure and feeling like a blast of arctic wind. Maybe like a woman with long mahogany hair.

Lurking . . . then suddenly sweeping down . . .

She's going to *kill* them. They're completely defenseless. . . .

Fear tore into Thea like jagged metal.

It was all happening right now, and she wasn't doing anything to stop it. It had been happening for almost an hour, and she hadn't even given it a thought.

CHAPTER
15

"Thea." Dani was shaking her arm. "They're *talking* to you."

The visions were gone. Thea was standing in Gran's workshop, seeing everything as if through a distorting lens. People's faces seemed to stretch; their voices seemed to drag.

"I *asked*, how did you learn the invocation for summoning spirits?" Gran said slowly.

Eric. He won't wait; he'll start without me. Or will he? I told him not to. But he'll be worrying about the party. . . .

The party. All those kids . . . even *little* kids. Humans, but *people*. Like baby chicks with a hawk up above. How many of them will end up like Kevin?

"The invocation for summoning spirits!" Gran was shouting, as if Thea were hard of hearing.

"I . . . we . . . *I* heard you at Samhain two years

ago. In Vermont. I saw the summoning the Inner Circle did." Even her own voice sounded weird and distorted.

"*We* saw you. Both of us. We were hiding behind the trees and you never even noticed," Blaise said clearly, and the bells rang again.

Dimly, Thea felt appreciation. But most of her mind was reeling from horrible thought to thought.

Eric . . . but if I try to get to him, if the Inner Circle finds out he's involved . . . *that* will get him killed. A human who knows about the Night World. Immediate death sentence.

But Suzanne. If he burns those dummies, Suzanne will kill him the way she killed Kevin.

No matter what happened, Eric was going to end up dead.

Unless . . .

"Which . . . of the spirits . . . did you call?" Gran was shouting, as if Thea was now not only hard of hearing but slow of understanding.

Unless . . .

"That's what I want to tell you," Thea said.

She could see the way. It would mean the end for her, but she might possibly save Eric. If there was enough time, if they would let her alone, if Eric wasn't right now trying to be a hero. . . .

"I *want* to tell you about it," Thea said again. And then the words were tumbling out in a rush, faster and faster, as if some dam had broken inside her. "And I'll tell you everything—but *please*, Grandma, *please*, you have to let me go out now. Just for a little while. There's something I have to do. You *have* to let me go, and then I'll come back here and you can do whatever you want to me."

"Hold on a minute," Mother Cybele said, but Thea couldn't stop.

"Please—*please*, Grandma. I've done a terrible thing—and I'm the only one who can take care of it. I'll come back—"

"Wait, wait, wait. Calm down," Gran said. She looked agitated herself. "What's this rush all of sudden? Try it slowly. What do you think you have to do?"

"I have to put her *back*." Thea saw that she was going to have to give some explanation. She tried to speak clearly and slowly, to make them understand. "The spirit I let out, Grandma. Her name is Suzanne Blanchet and she was burned in the sixteen hundreds. And she's out, out *there*, and she's already killed a human."

Everyone was listening now, some leaning forward, some frowning. Thea looked around at the circle of faces, talking to all of them. She was still terrified, but what did that matter? Eric mattered.

"Last week she killed a boy at my high school. And tonight she's going to kill more people, at the high school Halloween party. I can't explain how I know—there isn't *time*. But I do know. And I'm the only one who can stop her. I called her; I'm the only one who can put her back."

"Yes, but unfortunately it's not that easy," a low voice said. Thea turned and identified Rhys, a wiry man in a white lab coat. "If the spirit's at large—"

"I know about that, but I have a way to trap her.

SPELLBINDER

It's all set up, and I . . ." Thea hesitated. "I've tricked somebody into helping me," she said slowly. "And he's in danger right now. Which is why you have to let me go, let me take care of this. *Please.*"

"You want to go to the high school, where the party is," Aunt Ursula said. Although her lips were as thin as ever, she didn't sound angry. More—astute.

Thea opened her mouth to say no, and then stopped, confused again.

The party—or the desert? If Suzanne was really killing people at the party, she should go there. But only if Eric wasn't doing something to attract Suzanne to the desert. He was still more important to her than anyone else. But if he *wasn't* doing something—and if Suzanne was at the party—she might kill before Thea and Eric could lure her. . . .

I'm going crazy.

She felt, literally, as if she might faint. Her head was swimming. There were too many possibilities. It all depended on where Suzanne was right now, and there was no way to know that.

Thea began to shake violently, black dots dancing in front of her eyes.

I don't know what to do.

"I'm sorry . . . could everybody listen for a moment? I'm seeing something."

It was Aradia's voice, quiet and gently self-possessed. Mature, even though she was only a little older than Thea. Thea tried to see her through the black dots.

"I think it's something important, something about what we're talking about," Aradia said. Her beautiful

197

face, with its smooth skin the color of coffee with cream, was turned toward Thea. Her wide brown eyes looked straight ahead without focus, the way they always did.

Aradia couldn't see with those eyes—but then she didn't need to. She saw with her mind—and saw things that were hidden to most people.

"I'm seeing a boy—he's dressed in some old-fashioned costume. He's beside a fire, inside a circle of stones."

Eric. . . .

"He's got a stick—an ember. He's looking around. Now he's going to . . . it looks like a scarecrow. I can't see it well. There's a pile of sticks underneath it. He's bending. He's lighting the sticks."

No.

"I have to go," Thea said. She wasn't asking permission anymore.

Aradia was still speaking. "Okay, the sticks are catching fire. Now I can see better . . . and it's not a scarecrow; it looks sort of like a witch. A doll." She stopped, her lovely blind eyes widening. "It's—and it's moving—no, there's something moving it. I can see it now—a spirit. A spirit is moving the doll. It's coming out now—toward the boy—"

"I have to go," Thea said. And then she was moving, pushing her way between Rhys and Old Bob, breaking out of the circle. The beads of the curtain struck her face, clattering as they fell back behind her.

"Thea, wait a minute!"

"Thea, come back here!"

"Ursula, you go get her—"

The jeep. My backpack's in the *jeep*. I have to get it first.

The keys to the Lincoln were hanging on a nail by the back door. Thea grabbed them.

She pushed the back door open just as three or four people came hurrying through the bead curtain. She slammed the door in their faces.

Get to the car. *Fast.* Now drive.

She backed out of the alley, tires squealing. She could see light spill as the door to the shop opened, but by then she was turning onto Barren Street.

Eric . . .

She found herself driving at some new level, squeezing through the tail end of yellow lights, recognizing shortcuts in the dark. In just a few minutes she was at the Night World club with the jack-o'-lanterns on the porch.

There was no place to park the Lincoln. She left it in the middle of the street, with the keys still in the ignition. She pulled the key to the jeep out of her belt and jumped in.

Hurry. Hurry. She burned rubber again getting the jeep moving.

Hurry. The freeway.

Eric . . .

Just let me get to him. And let it not be too late. That's all I ask, after that I don't care.

Would you give up everything?

The voice didn't seem like a stranger this time, didn't seem menacing. Just curious. And Thea had an answer.

Yes.

If I can just get there, in time, I can send him away. I can tell him some story, make him go somehow. Make him hide. I'll tell the Circle I tricked him or enchanted him into helping; I won't even tell them his name. They can't make me.

Whatever they do to me, he'll be safe. That's all I care about. That's all I'm asking.

But even that was a lot, and she knew it, so she kept her foot mashed down on the gas pedal.

Freeway off ramp. Side road.

She drove crazily fast. The pounding inside her head kept saying hurry, hurry, even as she was careening off curbs.

Desert.

Now the road was bad. It was hard to see; the moon was almost down. The jeep lunged over bumps and lurched into potholes.

Eric, be doing something. Be talking to her, be running. You're so smart, please, please, be smart now. Keep her distracted, keep her hair away from your neck.

How strong was a spirit? Thea didn't know.

Please, I see everything so clearly now. I've been selfish, only thinking of me, what would make me happy. All that "encased in ice" garbage. I should have been dancing in the street. As long as Eric is all right, I don't care if he lives on Mars, I don't care if I never see him again. As long as he's well I'm happier than anybody has a right to be.

A jolt rattled her teeth. She was off the road now, driving by landmarks. Through forests of dead yuccas that looked like skinny gray Cousin Its.

It's taking so long, it's too long. Hurry. *Hurry.*

She could see red sandstone in front of her. Pillars in the headlights.

That's it! Go, go!

The jeep rocketed over clumps of blackbrush. She could see fire in the depression between the pillars. She drove straight toward it.

Fire—movement—the top of a silhouette . . .

"Eric!"

She was yelling even as she slammed on the brakes. The jeep ground to a shuddering stop a few inches from a misshapen sandstone tower.

"Eric!" She had the backpack in her hand. She tore the door open and jumped out, running.

"Thea! Stay out of here!"

She saw him.

The light of the fire cast an eerie glow onto the already lurid sandstone. Everything seemed red, as if this place were bathed in blood. The roar of the jeep's engine and the roar of the fire merged to sound like the flames of hell.

But Eric was alive and fighting. Fighting *it.*

Thea threw herself at it, even as her brain was registering impressions.

A wraith shape that looked at one second like a woman, and the next second like tattered clouds. Part of it seemed to be coiled around Eric, and he had both hands at his throat. Bits of the pine-needle amulet Thea had made for him were scattered around his feet. Useless.

"Get away from him! I'm the one who set this up!" Thea screamed. She reached Eric and grabbed wildly at the wraith, at the part of it around his throat. Her hands felt Eric's hands, felt cold air.

"No—Thea, watch out—"

She saw the thing come free of Eric, who staggered. She saw it re-form, gather, then dive straight for her.

"Thea!" Eric knocked her sideways. Cold air rushed by.

She and Eric fell in a heap.

She gasped "Eric, go," even before she got up. She tried to shove at him, looking around for the wraith. "Go—get out of here! The jeep's running—get in and just *drive*. I'll call you later."

"Stay back to back," Eric said breathlessly. "She's incredibly fast." He added through his teeth, "You know I'm not leaving."

"This is witch stuff, you jerk!" she snarled, standing back to back. "I don't *want* you. You'll just get in my way!"

It was a valiant effort. She even managed to inject something like hatred into her voice. And Eric wasn't perfect. He turned around, grabbed her by the shoulder, and yelled, *"You know I'm not going, so don't waste any more time!"*

Then he shoved her sideways again and freezing wind streaked by her cheek, leaving her ear numb.

"Sorry," he said in his normal voice. "You okay?"

Thea spun and looked behind her. The wraith was bobbing there. It was shaped like a woman made of vapor, with arms and legs only suggested, but with a long tail of hair that whipped around.

"I've got the stuff," Thea muttered to Eric. Admit-

ting she knew he'd never leave. "But it'll take a few minutes to do the spell. We'll have to keep out of—"

She was watching the lashing tail, but she wasn't fast enough. There was a sound—something between the snap of a whip and the crackle of electricity—and the tail flashed out. It was around her neck.

At first it just felt cold. Insubstantial but icy, like a scarf of subzero wind. But then the wraith gave a jerk and it tightened and it *did* have substance. It felt like metal, like a pipe full of supercooled liquid, like the tentacle of some alien creature with ice for blood. It was choking her.

She couldn't breathe and she couldn't get her fingers under it. It squeezed tighter, hurting her. She could feel her eyes start to bulge.

"Look at me!" Eric yelled. He had a stick that was blazing at one end and he was dancing up and down like a crazy person on the other side of the fire. "Look! Suzanne! I'm going to get your little sister!" He poked the burning stick at the dummy Lucienne, not at the wood piled around her, but at the actual doll.

"There! There! How do you like that?" He jabbed at the doll. A ring of fire blossomed in the black clothes. "Confess you're a witch!"

Thea felt something slide away and her neck was free.

She tried to shout a warning to Eric, but all that came out was a croak. He was already diving to one side anyway.

That must be what he's been doing all this time. Dodging.

"Eric, keep it up!"

"Okay, but work fast!" He threw himself the other way.

She forced herself to turn her attention from him. Her backpack was at the edge of the circle where she'd dropped it. She grabbed it and dumped the contents out on the ground.

She had to do this right and she had to do it faster than she'd ever worked a spell before.

Oak and ash. She threw them on the central fire, then scooted toward it, dragging the other materials close with a sweep of her arm.

She ripped open a plastic bag and grabbed the quassia chips. They were light, and she had to thrust her hand into the flames to make sure they actually went in the fire. Blessed thistle was powder; she threw it. Mandrake root was solid, she threw it, too.

She had just grabbed the ounce vial when Eric shouted, "Thea, *duck*."

She didn't look up to see what she was ducking. She fell flat instantly. It saved her. Icy wind blew her hair almost into the fire.

"Suzanne!" Eric was yelling. "I've got your brother! Look!"

There were fires at all three stakes now, and Eric was dashing between them, poking at one figure after another.

Thea pulled the plastic cap off the vial with her teeth. She shook it into the fire, her hand in the flames again.

One, two, *three*.

The fire roared up, louder than ever, and pure blue. Thea fell back from it.

"Suzanne! Over here!" Eric's voice was faint beyond the roar.

Tears were running down Thea's face, her nose and eyes stinging from the acrid smell. She fumbled for the last object necessary for the sending-back . . . the bag of residue from the bronze bowl. She took a handful in her left hand and dropped it between two charcoaled logs at the edge of the fire.

Then she stood up—and saw that Eric was in trouble.

He'd lost his burning stick. The wraith had him by the throat and it was whirling him around, changing shape every second. His mouth was open, but Thea couldn't hear any sound.

"May I be given the Power of the Words of Hecate!"

She *screamed* it, into the roaring fire, toward the wheeling, changing spirit shape.

And the words came, rolling off her tongue with a power of their own:

"From the heart of the flame . . . I send you back! Through the narrow path . . . I send you back!"

She put all her own power into the words, too, screaming them with an authority that she'd never felt in herself before. Because the wraith was *fighting*. It didn't want to go anywhere.

"To the airy void . . . I send you back! Through the mist of years . . . I send you back!"

Eric staggered, was jerked sideways. He seemed to be lifted off his feet by the wraith.

"To beyond the veil . . . I send you back! Go speedily, conveniently, and without delay!"

Eric's feet were kicking in the air. This is how Kevin died, Thea realized suddenly and with absolute certainty.

She found herself yelling words she'd never heard before. "By the power of Earth and Air and Water! By the power of Fire on this night of Hecate! By my own power as a daughter of Hellewise! *Go speedily, conveniently and without delay, you bitch!*"

She had no idea where *that* came from. But the next instant Eric fell. The wraith had dropped him.

It shot toward Thea—but then it stopped as if it had slammed into an invisible brick wall. It was directly over the fire.

Caught.

The blue flames were belching smoke—but sideways. Thea could see the wraith clearly above them. And for the first time, it didn't look like a cloud shape. It looked like a woman.

A girl. Older than Thea, but still in her teens. With long dark hair that floated around her and a pale face and huge sad eyes. Her lips were parted as if she were trying to speak.

Thea stared. She heard herself whisper, "Suzanne . . ."

The girl held out a pale hand toward her. But at the same moment the fire flared up again. It seemed to turn the girl's hair to fire, too. Dark fire was burning all around her and there was an expression of infinite sadness on her face.

Thea reached out a hand instinctively—

The fire roared—

And there was a flash like lightning.

Suzanne had been drawn to the heart of the flame. And now the lightning formed a cone: the narrow path.

Plastic bags and other debris whipped around the circle as if caught in a whirlwind.

Suzanne and the cone of white lightning disappeared into each other.

To the airy void. Through the mist of years.

The fire flared up above Thea's head, and then sank down. The blue seemed to fall to the bottom. The flames turned yellow, like ordinary fire.

It was as if a curtain had been drawn.

To beyond the veil.

That was where Suzanne was now.

At the edge of the bonfire, where the residue had been, there was a lump of soft clay. Thea knelt and picked it up. She looked into the center of the flames—and saw a coil of long hair, the color of mahogany. The ends were starting to blacken and shrink in the fire.

Thea reached in to grab it. She folded the hair over and quickly pressed the clay around it. It was a clumsy job, Blaise would have done much better, but the hair was enclosed. She groped on the ground for the wooden seal, found it, punched it into the clay. Suzanne's symbol, the cabalistic sign for her name, was printed.

It was done.

The amulet was restored, Suzanne was trapped again. She'd stay where she belonged unless somebody else was stupid enough to summon her.

Thea dropped the amulet without looking at it, got up, and staggered around the fire to where Eric was lying. Her vision was strangely gray.

After all this . . . he has to be all right . . . oh, please, let him be . . .

He moved when she reached him.

"Eric, we did it. She's gone. *We did it.*"

He grinned faintly. Said in a scratchy voice, "You don't have to cry."

She hadn't realized she was.

Eric sat up. He was terminally mussed, his hair wild, his face dirty. He looked wonderful to her.

"We did it," she whispered again. She reached out to smooth his hair, and her hand stayed there.

He glanced at the fire, then back at her. "I kind of hated to say those things to her. I mean, no matter how bad she was . . ." He touched Thea's neck, stroking gently. "Are you okay? I think you've got a bruise."

"Me? You're the one who really got it." She put her free hand to his throat, fingers just barely touching. "But I know what you mean," she whispered. "I felt—sorry—for her at the end."

"Don't cry again. Please. I really hate that," he whispered, and he put *his* free arm around her.

And then they were just kissing madly. Deliriously. Laughing and kissing and holding each other. She could taste her own tears on his lips, warming with his warmth, and she was trembling like a bird in a thicket.

A few moments later a noise broke in. Thea didn't want to move, but Eric looked, and then he stiffened.

"Uh, we've got company."

Thea looked up.

There were cars just outside the sandstone pillars. Parked cars. They must have driven up sometime during the fight with Suzanne, while the roar of the fire blocked out the sound of their engines, while Thea's attention was focused on the wraith trying to kill her.

Because the people were already out of the cars. Grandma Harman, supported by Aunt Ursula. Rhys in his lab coat. Dumpling-shaped Mother Cybele, with her hand on Aradia's arm. Old Bob, Nana Buruku.

Most of the Inner Circle was here.

CHAPTER

16

Thea started to let go of Eric. She could still try to save him.

But *he* wouldn't let go. And her own instincts told her to hold on to him.

They stood up together, holding each other, facing the Inner Circle as a unit.

"Well," Mother Cybele said, blinking rapidly. "Aradia brought us here thinking you might need help. But you've taken care of things yourselves. We saw the end, very impressive."

"I saw it, too," Aradia said. Her face was turned toward Thea, the faintest trace of a smile on her lips. "You did a good job, Thea Harman. You're a true Hearth-Woman."

"Yes, and where did that last invocation come from?" Gran said, shifting her weight to the cane Rhys gave her. "I've never in my life heard of anybody calling on their own power as a daughter of Hellewise." She said it in a grumbling way, but Thea had the strange feeling that she was almost pleased.

Thea faced them all, Maiden, Mother, and Crone of the Inner Circle. She was still holding Eric. "I don't know where it came from," she said, and was glad to hear that her voice wasn't shaking too badly. "It just . . . came."

"And what about you? What's your name, young man?" Gran said.

"Eric Ross." Thea was proud of the way he said it, quiet and respectful, but not cowed.

Gran looked from him to Thea. And back again.

"You're in this with my granddaughter?"

"He doesn't know anything. . . ." Thea began, but of course that was hopeless. And ridiculous.

"I know I love Thea," Eric said, cutting her off. "And she loves me. And if there's some rule that says we can't be together, it's a stupid rule."

He sounded terribly brave and terribly young. Thea felt a wave of dizziness. Her fingers tightened on his until both their hands were shaking from the pressure. She realized for the first time that her right hand was fairly seriously burned.

"Please let him go, Grandma," she whispered. And then, as Gran stood silent, "Please . . . I won't ever see him again and he won't ever tell. All he's done is try to help me, try to save lives. *Please* don't punish him for what's my fault." Warmth pooled in her eyes and spilled over.

"He tried to uphold the law," Aradia said. "At least, I think so."

Thea wasn't sure she'd heard right. Gran didn't seem to be, either. She said, "How's that?"

"Hellewise said it's forbidden for witches to kill humans, didn't she?" Aradia asked, her face serene. "Well, that spirit was a witch who'd already killed a human—and who wanted to kill more. And he helped send her back. He helped Thea undo the forbidden spell, and he helped prevent witch law from being broken again."

Rhys muttered, "Neatly put," but Thea couldn't tell whether that meant that he agreed or not.

Gran shuffled a step forward, looking at Eric. "And just what did you do to help, young man?"

"I don't know if I *did* help," Eric said in his quiet, straightforward way. "Mainly I just tried to keep her from killing me—"

"When did you light the fires?" Thea asked in an undertone, still clutching his hands.

He glanced at her. One side of his mouth quirked slightly.

"Nine o'clock," he said.

"Even though I wasn't there." Thea's voice was just slightly louder now. "And you knew Suzanne would come and try to get you, and you didn't have any magic to fight her. So why did you do it?"

He looked at her, then at Gran. Then at her. "You know why. Because otherwise she'd have gone over to the party."

"And killed more people." Thea looked at Gran.

Gran was staring at Eric, her dark old eyes very keen. "So you saved lives."

"I don't know," Eric said again, maddeningly honest. "But I didn't want to take the chance."

"He saved my life, too," Thea said. "Suzanne tried to kill me. And I could never have gotten through the spell to send her back if he hadn't kept her distracted."

"That's nice, but I'm not sure it's enough," Old Bob said, running a hand over his stubbly chin. His weathered face was quizzical. "There's nothing that says upholding one law makes up for breaking another. Especially Night World law. We could get in a mess of trouble fooling with that."

Gran and Mother Cybele looked at each other. Then Gran turned to Old Bob.

"I changed your diapers—don't tell me you know more about Night World law," she snapped. "I'm not about to let a bunch of bloodthirsty vampires dictate to me." She looked at the others. "We need to take this somewhere private. Let's go back to my place."

Somewhere private. Hope kept racing giddily through Thea as the jeep bounced and rattled home.

Eric was driving, and Thea was in the backseat, so they couldn't talk. Aunt Ursula was in the front beside Eric.

Gran's fighting for me. And Aradia, and maybe even Mother Cybele. They don't want me to die. I don't think they even want Eric to die.

But reality kept trying to push the hope away.

What can they do? They can't condone a witch and a human being together. They can't risk war with the rest of the Night World, not even to save me.

There's no solution.

The little caravan pulled up the back alley behind Gran's store.

And then Thea was in the workshop again, in the circle of chairs. Creon and Belfana had been waiting. So had Blaise and Dani, who were both sitting down.

"Are you okay?" Dani began, standing—and then she shut up. She was looking at Eric, her dark, velvety eyes huge. A human in the Circle.

"We put Suzanne back," Thea said simply. She took Eric's hand again.

The Inner Circle re-formed around the two of them, witch and human, standing centered.

"We have a situation," Gran said. And she explained even though most of them already understood the problem. She did it thoroughly, looking at each of the Circle members in turn. Aradia and Mother Cybele sat on either side of her, occasionally putting in a thoughtful remark.

Thea figured it out in a few minutes. Gran was recruiting each of them, appealing to them—and showing that the Mother and Maiden both agreed with her. She was working them all over to her side.

"And the end result is, we've got these two," she said at last. "And we have to decide what to do with them. This is a decision for the Inner Circle, for the daughters and sons of Hellewise. *Not* for the Night World Council," she added, looking at Old Bob.

He ran a hand through rough gray hair and muttered, "The Council might not see it just that way," But he smiled.

"There was a time," Gran said, "when witches and

humans got along better than they do now. I'm sure anybody who's gone far enough back with their family tree knows that."

Eric looked at Thea, who shook her head and looked at Blaise.

"She means," Mother Cybele put in, "that we used to take human husbands, a long time ago. To make up for the fact that there have never been enough witch men. That was back in the days when there was still the third Circle, Circle Daybreak. The one that tried to teach magic to humans."

"Until humans started burning us," Belfana said, her freckled face grave under its coil of deep red hair.

"Well, *this* one isn't likely to burn anybody," Aunt Ursula said acidly. At that moment, Thea loved her.

"Nobody is arguing that the laws should be changed," Mother Cybele said, putting her plump fingers together. "We can't go back to those days, and we all know the danger from humans now. The question is, is there any way to make an exception in this one case?"

"I don't see how," Rhys said slowly. "Not without all of us ending up accused of treason."

"It'll be the Night Wars all over again," Nana Buruku added. "Each race of Night People against the others."

"I don't wish them harm," Creon said from his wheelchair, his cracked voice barely audible. "But they can't live in our world, and they can't live in the human world."

And that, Thea thought, sums it up perfectly. There

is no place for us. Not while one of us is witch and the other is human. . . .

The idea came in a single flash, like the lightning from the balefire.

So simple. And yet so terrifying.

It might work. . . .

But if it did, could I stand it?

Would you give up everything?

Everything—including Gran and Blaise. Dani and Lawai'a and Cousin Celestyn. Uncle Galen, Aunt Gerdeth, Aunt Ursula . . . Selene and Vivienne, everybody at Circle Twilight.

The smell of herbs, lavender mixed with rose petals. The kiss of cool stones in her palm. Every chant, every invocation . . . all the spells she'd learned. The feel of magic flowing through her fingertips. Even the memory of Hellewise . . .

Hellewise in her white shift, in the dark forest . . .

Would you give up everything . . . for peace?

For Eric?

This time the inner voice was her own. She found herself looking at Eric and knowing she already had her answer.

He was so good, so dear. Tender but intense. Smart and brave and honest and insightful . . . and loving.

He loves me. He was willing to die for me.

He'd give up everything.

Eric was watching her, his gray-flecked eyes concerned. He could tell that something was going on with her.

Thea smiled at him. And was so proud to see that even now, surrounded by people who must seem like figures from some horrible legend to him, he could give her a wry half-smile back.

"I have an idea," she said to Gran and the Inner Circle. "The Cup of Lethe."

There was a silence. People looked at each other. Gran was startled.

"Not just for him," Thea said. "For me."

Long breaths quietly drawn in the silence.

Gran shut her eyes.

"If I drank enough, I'd forget everything," Thea forged on, talking to all the grave faces. "Everything about the Night World. I wouldn't be a witch anymore, because I wouldn't remember who I am."

"You'd become a lost witch," Aradia said. Her lovely face was calm, not appalled. "Like the psychics who don't know their heritage. And lost witches can live with humans."

"And neither of us would remember about the Night World," Thea said. "So how could we be breaking any laws?"

"The law would be satisfied," Aradia said.

Eric's hand tightened on Thea's. "But—"

She looked at him. "It's the only way for us to be together."

He shut his mouth.

This silence was very long.

Then Blaise, who had been standing with crossed arms, watching, said, "She told *me* they were soulmates."

For an instant, Thea thought she was saying it spitefully, to harm.

But Gran was turning in surprise. "Soulmates. That's a notion I haven't heard in a while."

"An archaic myth," Rhys said, shifting in his lab coat.

"Maybe not," Mother Cybele said softly. "Maybe the old powers are waking up again. Maybe they're trying to tell us something."

Gran looked down at the floor. When she looked back at Thea, there were tears in her fierce dark eyes. And for the first time since Thea had known her, those eyes looked truly old.

"If we did let you do this," she said, "if we let you renounce your heritage and walk away from us . . . where would you go?"

It was Eric who answered. "With me," he said simply. "My mom and my sister already love her. And my mom knows she's an orphan. If I tell her Thea can't stay here anymore—well, she'd take her in, no questions."

"I see," Gran said. Eric hadn't mentioned that his mom already thought Thea was living in an unstable home with an unbalanced old lady, but Thea had the feeling Gran knew.

Another pause, as Gran looked around the Circle. Finally, she nodded and let out a breath. "I think the girl's given us a way out," she said. "Does anybody disagree?"

No one spoke. Most of the faces were pitying. *They think it's a fate worse than death,* Thea realized.

Blaise said suddenly, "I'll get the Cup."

She clashed through the bead curtain.

Good. It's good to get it over with, Thea thought. Her

heart was pounding wildly. She and Eric were holding hands so tightly that her burned fingers stung.

"It won't hurt," she whispered to him. "We'll be sort of confused . . . but it should come back to us . . . except anything about magic."

"You can transfer into zoology," he said. "And go to Davis." He was smiling, but his eyes were full.

Dani stepped forward. "Can I . . . I'd just like to say good-bye." She got through that much steadily. Then she choked and threw herself into Thea's arms.

Thea hugged back. "I'm sorry I got you in trouble," she whispered.

"You didn't—you told them it wasn't my fault. They're not going to do anything to me. But it's going to be so lonely at school without you . . ." Dani stepped away, shaking her head, trying not to cry. "Blessed be."

Blaise was back, little bells ringing. She had a pewter chalice in one hand and a bottle in the other.

Just seeing the bottle sent a shiver through Thea. The glass was so dark with age she couldn't tell what color it had been originally, and so misshapen it was hard to know if it was meant to be round or square. There was wax over the cork and all sorts of seals and ribbons.

Gran broke through the seals, pulled off the ribbons. She tried to twist the cork out of the wax, but Blaise had to help.

Then she tipped the bottle above the cup Blaise held.

Brownish liquid ran out. Gran poured until the cup was half full.

"When you drink this," Gran said to Thea, "you'll

forget me. You won't know anyone here. But we won't forget you." She spoke formally, an announcement before the Circle. "Thea Sophia Harman, let the record show that you are a true daughter of Hellewise."

She shuffled forward and kissed Thea's cheek.

Thea hugged her, feeling the fragile old body for the last time. "Good-bye, Gran. I love you."

Then Blaise came, offering the cup in both hands. She looked wild and beautiful, her hair a cataract of black tumbling around her, her hands pale around the chalice.

"Good-bye," Thea said, and took it from her.

Blaise smiled.

Now, Thea told herself. Don't hesitate. Don't *think* about it.

She lifted the cup to her lips and drank.

And choked slightly on the first swallow. It was— it tasted like . . .

Her eyes went to Blaise's.

Which were large and gray and luminous. They looked at her steadily. So steadily that it was a warning.

Thea kept drinking.

Tea. Watered-down iced tea. *That* was what the Cup of Lethe tasted like.

That bottle was sealed—she didn't have time— there was wax on the cork . . .

Thea's mind was churning. But she had enough sense to do one thing—she drank a *lot* of whatever was in the cup, so there wouldn't be any left over for the Circle to examine when Eric was done.

And she kept her face blank as Blaise took the chalice from her and gave it to Eric.

Eric drank, looked slightly surprised, and kept drinking.

"Finish it *allll*," Blaise said. Her eyes were still on Thea's.

And that was when Thea knew for sure.

You did it before, when you were first talking about giving human boys the Cup of Lethe after spilling their blood at the Homecoming dance. You poured it out and stashed it somewhere and put in tea and redid all those seals—of course *you* could reproduce them with molds. And now . . . and now . . .

As Blaise took the chalice back from Eric, it hit Thea in a wave that almost made her hysterical.

This is never going to work. They're never going to *believe* it. But . . .

Thea took Eric's hand and sank her nails into his palm. She didn't dare say a word to him, didn't dare even look at him. But she was thinking, don't speak, don't do *anything*, just follow my lead.

She made her face as blank as a wax doll.

Eric was just standing there. He didn't know what to expect, but he obviously felt Thea's nails. And he proved how smart he was by not speaking.

"We stand adjourned," Gran said tersely. "Blaise, take them out while they're still confused. They should be able to get home on their own." She turned away without looking at Thea.

"No problem," Blaise said.

Aradia said, "I'll go with you."

CHAPTER

17

They walked out to Eric's jeep. The night air was very cold and there was no moon.

Thea kept her hand on Eric's back, ready to press if he hesitated. But he never did.

At the door of the jeep, Thea looked at Blaise. She was afraid to show any expression. Could Aradia see them? She wanted desperately to give Blaise a last hug.

Aradia said, "Is there a window from the shop onto this street?"

Thea looked at Blaise. Blaise said, "No."

"Then you can say good-bye. After this you're going to have to pretend not to know each other."

Thea stared at her, then felt a wild choked giggle well up. "Now I know why you're Maiden," she said, in a bare whisper. "But—does anyone else realize?"

"I don't think so. Some may wonder, but I think they'll keep their mouths shut. Say good-bye quick."

Thea hugged Blaise, couldn't make herself let go. "Thank you. Oh, Eileithyia, Blaise, I'll miss you."

"Now *I'm* the last of the Harman line," Blaise said in a bad imitation of a smirking voice. "I'll have a bedroom to myself," she added in more believable tones. "And I'm going to get Sheena good."

"Who?"

"That's right, you didn't hear. She was the one who turned us in. She's one of Tobias's little girl-friends, Circle Midnight. It seems he's been spying on us. He told her enough that she understood we were doing forbidden spells, and she told Gran."

"It doesn't matter now."

"Are you kidding? I'm getting sent to the Convent. I'm going to *kill* her." The bells rang as Blaise tossed her head.

Then she tightened her grip on Thea. "I don't know why you want to be with a human," she whispered. "But I hope you keep on wanting it now that you have it."

"Blaise, when you get back—please don't hurt them anymore. They're people. Really."

Blaise sighed noncommittally; Thea could feel it. But all she said, almost too softly for Thea to hear, was, "I'll miss you—sister."

Then Thea could let go.

When she was in the jeep, Aradia leaned into the open door.

"Two things," she said rapidly. "And they're all the help I can give you. Mother Cybele mentioned Circle Daybreak. I've heard rumors that there are witches somewhere who are starting it up again, witches who want to forget the Burning Times, and who don't hold to Night World law. I don't know if it's true. But if it is, maybe you can find it."

Thea's breath was taken away. The possibility leaped inside her like some unimagined joy.

"And the other thing," Aradia said, with a rare smile—almost a brief grin. "Word is that some of your Redfern cousins have started going peculiar. I've even heard that they're talking about finding human soulmates, just like you. You might try and contact *them* and see what the story is."

Thea's breath came back, and with it, tears. "Oh, Aradia. Thank you."

"Good luck, Thea. And Eric. Both of you, wherever you go."

Eric, who had been sitting quietly behind the wheel, reached out to touch her hand lightly. "And you, too." Thea could tell by his voice that he was puzzled and dazed, but he was trying not to show it.

Then they drove away. Thea turned around to watch Blaise getting smaller and smaller. A little wind blew Blaise's hair, and she looked like a dark and mysterious Aphrodite, a goddess who always did what you least expected.

Eric drove fast until they were a good distance from the shop, then pulled to the curb on a tiny residential street. He looked at Thea and said cautiously, "Am I immune to *this* stuff? Because I'm not forgetting anything. Or is it going to kick in any minute now?"

Thea kissed him.

Then she began to laugh hysterically.

"No. No."

"You mean we're really safe? You're going to keep your powers?"

"Yes! Yes!"

She had to keep telling him over and over to convince him. But finally he got it and his face changed. Was transformed by his lightning-bolt smile. He squeezed her and shook her and finally jumped out of the jeep and yelled "All right! Way to go, Blaise! *All right! Yes!*"

"Eric!"

He pounded the jeep.

"Eric, get back in, you idiot! There might be Night People around." Then, still laughing uncontrollably with love and gratitude and the relief of tension, she said, "Come in *here*." And she held out her arms.

He jumped back in. They fit together perfectly, his arms around her, his breath against her hair.

"I'm so happy," he said. "I love you, witch."

Thea was laughing and crying at once. "I love you, too."

He kissed her temple. She kissed his cheek. Then he kissed her mouth and stayed there for a long while. And Thea forgot about laughing, forgot that there was a world outside the two of them.

And then they sat together in the darkness, resting against each other, just breathing. Safe. Connected.

Thea was with someone who knew her, who saw what she saw. Her soulmate. And they were free to be with each other, without being hunted, without fear.

She was filled with joy and tranquility.

And with quiet sadness, too. It wasn't as if this new beginning came free. She still was an exile, cut off from her family. Gran was lost to her. If she saw Blaise, it would have to be in secret. She'd given up a lot. *Almost* everything.

But she didn't regret it. Not with Eric warm and solid in her arms. Not with the Night World saved from civil war, and the threat to the humans here over.

And what now? she wondered.

Strangely, even though there was no clear answer, she didn't feel afraid. She could visualize many futures, and they all seemed equally likely.

Now they would go to Eric's house, and Eric's mother would be puzzled but generous, and Roz would be ferocious but delighted. And next week Thea would go back to school and transfer into honors zoology.

She would get a scholarship to Davis and become a vet and use her powers to find out what was wrong with sick animals. Or she would find herself interested in wolves or elephants and would become a naturalist and visit faraway places to study them. Or she and Eric would adopt a puppy like Bud and write a book together to help people understand their dogs.

Or she would find Circle Daybreak and meet witches who wanted to forget the Burning Times. And they would be the first to reintroduce humans to magic, and Rosamund would grow up fierce and proud, knowing all the legends of Hellewise.

Or she would find her vampire cousins and see if the soulmate principle was really coming back. And their group would be like a magnet, attracting other young Night People with radical ideas, starting an underground revolution.

Maybe a new generation of Redferns and Harmans were forming alliances with humans. Maybe it was time for hatred to stop.

Maybe the old powers were waking and new times were coming. Maybe the world was about to change.

Only one thing was sure.

There were infinite possibilities.

She held Eric and felt his breathing and was at peace with the night.

ABOUT THE AUTHOR

LISA JANE SMITH is the author of more than a dozen books for young adults. She enjoys writing about strong female characters and encouraging girls to read, write, and reach for their dreams. A former teacher, she lives in the Bay area of northern California. Her Archway trilogies include *The Forbidden Game* and *Dark Visions*.

Don't miss the next

NIGHT WORLD™

Dark Angel

One day Gillian Lennox almost dies . . .
and is saved by an angel. When he
brings her back from her near-death experience, he says he's her guardian. But
soon he's guiding Gillian into the most
deadly danger. Who is Angel really?
What's his claim on Gillian? And why
is he drawing her into the depths of the
Night World? Gillian and her friend
David Blackburn have to find out before
it's too late. . . .

Enter The NIGHT WORLD™

SWEEPSTAKES!

There are two cardinal rules in the *Night World*: never to tell humans that it exists and never to fall in love with a human. The black flower is an important symbol of the *Night World* because it is how the members identify one another. You can be a member of The Black Rose, the secret club of the *Night World*, because now you can win a gold-plated flower pin or other terrific prizes by entering the *Night World*™ Sweepstakes.

One Grand Prize
A gold-plated flower pin like those worn in the *Night World*

Ten First Prizes
A *Night World*™ t-shirt

Fifteen Second Prizes
A glow-in-the-dark solar system sticker collection

Twenty-five Third Prizes
A *Night World*™ book autographed by L.J. Smith

An Archway Paperback Published by Pocket Books

Name_____

Birthdate_____

Address_____

City_____State_____Zip_____

Phone_____

1221(1of2)

See next page for official rules

ARCHWAY PAPERBACKS "Night World™" SWEEPSTAKES Official Rules:

1. No Purchase Necessary. Enter by submitting the completed Official Entry Form (no copies allowed) or by sending on a 3" x 5" card your name and address to the Archway Paperbacks/*Night World*™ Sweepstakes, Advertising and Promotion Department, 13th Floor, 1230 Avenue of the Americas, NY, NY 10020. Entries must be received by 4/25/97. Not responsible for lost, late or misdirected mail. Enter as often as you wish, but one entry per envelope. Winners will be selected at random from all entries received in a drawing to be held on or about 4/28/97.

2. Prizes: One Grand Prize: a gold-plated flower pin (approximate retail value: $25.00). Ten First Prizes: a *Night World*™ t-shirt, adult size large (approximate retail value: $10.00 each). Fifteen Second Prizes: a glow-in-the-dark solar system sticker collection (approximate retail value: $5.00 each). Twenty-five Third Prizes: a *Night World*™ book autographed by L.J. Smith (retail value: $3.99). All dollar amounts are U.S. dollars.

3. The sweepstakes is open to residents of the U.S. and Canada. Prizes will be awarded to the winner's parent or legal guardian if under 18. Void in Puerto Rico and wherever else prohibited by law. Employees of Viacom International, Inc., their suppliers, affiliates, agencies, participating retailers, and their families living in the same household are not eligible. Prizes are not transferable and may not be substituted. One prize per household. The odds of winning a prize depend upon the number of entries received. All prizes will be awarded.

4. If a winner is a Canadian resident, then he/she must correctly answer a skill-based question administered by mail. Any litigation respecting the conduct and awarding of a prize in this publicity contest may be submitted to the Regis des Loteries et Courses du Quebec.

5. All federal, state and local taxes are the responsibility of the winners. Winners will be notified by mail. Winners grant Archway Paperbacks the right to use their names, likenesses, and entries for any advertising, promotion and publicity purposes without further compensation to or permission from the entrants, except where prohibited by law. For a list of major prize winners (available after 4/28/97) send a stamped, self-addressed envelope to Prize Winners, Archway Paperbacks/*Night World*™ Sweepstakes, Advertising and Promotion Department, 13th Floor, 1230 Avenue of the Americas, NY, NY 10020.

Night World is a trademark of Lisa J. Smith.